**Other books by Deirdre Hutchins**

## The Paranormal Investigators League series

PIL #1  Voodoo in Savannah

PIL #2  A Hanging in Tucson

PIL #3  Suicide on Sunset

PIL #4  The Legend of Providence

PIL #5  Darkness in Denver

PIL #6  Spirits in Seattle

PIL Prequel: The Origin Story

## The Dark Prophecy trilogy

1: Resurrection of the Vampire

2: Vengeance of the Damned

3: Deliverance from the Prophecy

## The Daphne Winters Psychic Investigation Series

DW1  The Body and the Soul

DW2  Finding Maddy


These are all available from the San Joaquin Valley Press.

Visit us at www.sanjoaquinvalleypress.com

Daphne Winters Psychic Investigation Series
#3

# Dropped Dead

A Novel

By Deirdre Hutchins

San Joaquin Valley Press
Fresno, California

*Dropped Dead* is published by
    San Joaquin Valley Press
    P.O. Box 9485
    Fresno, CA  93792
    www.sanjoaquinvalleypress.com



Cover design by Andria Davis Kaye
The cover is a collage of elements from Shutterstock: Teenage Boy by Armin Staude; Highway Overpass by John_T

ISBN 978-1-7378061-9-6

# PROLOGUE

I'm wandering the streets by myself and it's late at night or very early morning.  I don't remember coming out here.  What was I looking for?  What am I doing here?  Where are my friends?

I've been down this road so many times before.  I know these shops.  I've seen these street signs.  But it's quiet right now.  Quieter than it should be.  There's an ominous cloud of oppression smothering everything as I drift on by.

I need to find someone I know.  I start to move faster, peering in every window and parked car.  There's no one.

At a stoplight up ahead in the distance I see a gathering of people.  There's no one near me because they are all up there for some reason.  They're standing in the street, pointing and gesturing toward the ground.

I know instantly that this is why I am here.

I start running toward the crowd, desperate to find the answers my mind is craving. I am drawn to this gathering with every fiber of my being.

As I get closer, the hum of the crowd starts to get louder. I can't make out any distinct words, but I know they are buzzing about whatever is on the ground. In the street. I need to see it. I need to know.

I start to push through the crowd, but I don't even need to. They part for me willingly.

It's a body, mangled and twisted in unnatural ways. I've never seen anything like it before. But that's not even what makes me freeze in horror. It's the face.

I know that face.

The body lying there in the middle of the street, dropped like it was nothing more than a dirty rag, is mine.

My human life has ended.

# 1.

"Just start from the beginning, Gina," Miguel told his partner.  It was his first Monday back after being on medical leave for a bullet to his shoulder.  It was still a little sore—and might be for a while—but he at least felt good enough for a desk job.

Besides, he'd never admit to The Sarge that he felt anything at all.  As far as everyone knew at the precinct, he was back full strength and raring to go.

Gina sighed and put her feet up on her desk, crossing them at the ankles.  She was dressed professionally, her hair pulled back, her make-up feminine and flawless.  "I told you.  Once Daphne does her psychic thing, we'll be able to move on from this one.

There are three more cases on our plates right now."

To emphasize the work overload, she took a pile of manila folders and plopped them unceremoniously on her desk. "And anyway, we're only doing this to make the family happy. It's a P.R. thing. The guy jumped to his death. Open-and-closed suicide case."

"Well, that's the thing. Daphne already had a feeling that wasn't true. She said he died *before* he got to the overpass. So someone dropped him after he was already dead. I want to know why." Miguel sipped his coffee and leaned back in his chair. He certainly respected that they had a never-ending caseload, and this one wasn't confirmed to be a homicide. Normally, he'd be the one nagging Gina to put it on the bottom.

But Daphne changed everything. Her misgivings gave him misgivings.

Without taking her feet off the desk, Gina folded her arms across her lap. "Did Daphne talk to the boy's ghost?"

Miguel shook his head. With his highly-styled

and very-gelled hairdo, not a hair moved, as usual. "Not yet."

Gina sighed. "Then let's at least see what progress we can make on the drive-by shooting in the Tower District. We can tackle the Ethan Bender case later."

"Is that his name? Ethan?"

Gina dug through the pile of manila folders she had just dropped on her desk moments ago. She found the one for Ethan Bender and handed it to Miguel. "Yes," she said. "Eighteen years old. Honor roll student. According to his parents, a jolly, happy soul. Everyone loved him, blah, blah, blah. They never believed it was a suicide from the word go."

Miguel frowned. Grieving parents of a young victim were always a painful part of the job. "It's hard to accept, I'm sure. But teenagers are also very adept liars. And keeping things from their parents is their special area of expertise."

"So what are you thinking?" Gina asked. She

raised an eyebrow on her perfectly made-up face.  She wore her long, brown hair back in a ponytail and, despite working in a male-dominated field, she always managed to look quite feminine.  Dressing neat and tidy was very important to Miguel, so he always respected Gina's effort to appear tough, but feminine and well put together.

"I'm not really thinking anything.  Just saying we treat this like any other investigation until we hear otherwise."

Gina lifted her feet off her desk and let them fall to the floor with a thud that echoed throughout the bull pen.  Lots of heads turned her way, and she smiled.  She loved that part almost as much as annoying The Sarge when she put her feet *on* the desk.

Pushing her hands off her thighs, she stood, towering over Miguel who was still seated at his desk.  "Then we can canvas the crime scene at Tower, and then Daphne can meet us where we found Ethan.  Maybe his ghost will appear, and we can give the family some peace of mind by lunch."

Miguel stood as well.  "Yeah, that would be fantastic."  He took another sip of his coffee before throwing what was left away in his desk trash can.

Gina lightly jabbed Miguel in the shoulder where he had been injured a few weeks back.  "How's the gunshot wound?"

Miguel couldn't hide the wince from the pain, but he recovered quickly.  "I'm fully healed."

Gina stared at him with a look of pure skepticism.  "Uh-huh."

"No, seriously.  You just caught me off guard is all."

"You were cleared for field work, though, right?"  One eyebrow raised, Gina folded her arms across her chest, daring him to lie to her.  She could read him like a book. And right now, she could probably kick his ass.

"I'm cleared."  This was true but he knew he had to come clean with Gina.  Lying to her was as useless as lying to Daphne. Both ladies could see right through him. "I might have put on a bit of extra bravado when I was being evaluated, but I was cleared for work.  I'm good.  Let's catch a drive-by shooter or two."

Gina rolled her eyes.  "You know it was a car full of tough guys," she said.

"Yeah.  The extra toughest ones never get out of their car as they mow you down and then speed off like the chicken shits they are."

Gina laughed at the image.

Working homicide in Fresno forced Gina and Miguel to face the worst of the worst in crime.  Murderers, drug dealers, domestic abusers…they'd seen it all.  But the common theme in all of them was, at the end of the day, there was always just a scared little person trying to be tough and things went too far.

She didn't feel sorry for them.  Far from it.  Gina was scared sometimes too, but she didn't go around killing people because of it.  No, she loved putting those cowards behind bars where they couldn't go around killing anyone else.  You get your shit together before you kill someone.  That was how Gina saw the world.

"When was our last drive-by?" Miguel asked, grabbing the keys. "Feels like it's been a while." He wore a white button-down shirt with his sleeves rolled up his forearm. In the cooler months, he would wear a sports jacket, but these summer months in Fresno were far too hot. It was triple digits today, so this was the best he could muster.

Gina looked to the ceiling, as if the answer would appear floating above her head. "Uh, yeah. It does seem like it's been longer than it should be. Maybe six months?"

"Maybe we're doing that good of a job cleaning up these streets."

Gina smiled at her partner. "You keep telling yourself that, Miguel."

"Alvarez! Malone!" The familiar voice of The Sarge echoed across the room. "Get in here."

A chorus of "oooh's" teased Miguel and Gina good-naturedly as they wandered over to his office. Gina rolled her eyes dramatically at her fellow law enforcers.

Miguel just ignored them.  He'd endured much worse in his time on the force.

"And just where do you think you're going?" The Sarge gruffed out the second Miguel closed the glass door behind him.  The bull pen could watch through the glass windows, and he could feel the eyes burning his backside from the onlookers.  He wouldn't dare give them the satisfaction of turning around.

"Tower District drive-by.  Heading to the scene," Gina explained with a shrug.

But The Sarge shook his head.  "Nope.  Miguel was cleared for desk duty.  You're now with Sheffley for field work."

"Bullshit!" Gina exclaimed before her brain could think it through.

But The Sarge wasn't worried about language. He ignored Gina and turned to Miguel.  "You.  Back to your desk."

"I feel great," Miguel answered.  He had said it so much he was starting to believe it, even though he could feel his shoulder smarting as he stood there.

"I don't give a shit if you could do a cartwheel right here in the office," The Sarge bellowed. "You're not cleared. Back to your desk." He pointed in the direction of Miguel's desk to add emphasis.

"Sheffley is too green, Sarge. He's barely out of diapers," Gina argued. "At least put me back with Ball."

"Then you can show him how to be ungreen. You don't make these calls. I do. Now back to it." The Sarge made a shooing motion with his hands indicating their discussion was over. Gina opened her mouth to argue again, but Miguel rested a hand on her elbow to stop her.

"It's okay. We can divide and conquer. You do Tower drive-by and I'll do Ethan Bender. From my desk." Miguel spoke softly to his partner, knowing full well The Sarge could hear everything.

"Fine." Gina pursed her lips in a manner that said she had much more to say but was keeping it to herself.

"Glad you're seeing reason. You're dismissed," The Sarge said with a huge condescending smile. Gina again fought the urge to retort, but then she thought better of it and followed Miguel out of the office.

Once they were out of earshot of the boss, Gina leaned in to her partner. "Sometimes I feel like we're surrounded by children."

Miguel huffed a laugh, but he was quickly distracted by his phone. "It's Daphne," he announced to Gina and then took the call. In no rush to grab her rookie partner, she stayed and listened to Miguel's "uh-huhs" and "okays" on this end of the conversation.

When he hung up, he smiled. Gina folded her arms as she waited for his update, one eyebrow raised in question.

He looked so smug Gina almost wanted to hit him as he whispered, "Guess who just visited Daphne."

# 2.

Daphne was no stranger to ghosts in her living room.

She sat in her bathrobe, short blonde hair disheveled from sleep. But who was she kidding? Her hair was always disheveled. In fact, until she'd met Miguel—and barely even then—she hadn't cared one iota what any living person thought about her.

Life was short and then you die and haunt psychics in the hereafter.

And she'd encountered many emotions from the intruders in those ghostly visits. Anger, jealousy, guilt, rage, worry. The emotions often came flying at her in a way that overwhelmed her senses and made it difficult for her to know if she was actually feeling those things, or if the ghost was projecting.  And the ghosts almost always appeared in the form that they had died in: mutilated, stabbed, blue from lack of oxygen.

But this ghost was different.

Ethan Bender stood before her like any average popular teenage boy.  At least, she assumed he was popular because he looked athletic and those types were always popular in high schools, according to movies. Daphne really had no idea.  She'd never been popular or paid any attention to who was at her high school.  She'd survived high school by avoiding as many people as she could until she could graduate.

Ethan was clean cut, dressed in a stylish way, and almost cheerful in disposition.

"What happened to you?"  Daphne got straight to the point.  Ethan might have all eternity, but Daphne needed to go grocery shopping.  Her little jaunt to Southern California to work on the cold case that changed her life had left her cupboard bare and food spoilt.

Ethan shrugged.  "You tell me.  One minute I'm leaving Jake's house.  The next everyone's crowded around my body in the middle of the street."

"So you didn't jump?"  Daphne plopped her slippered feet up on the coffee table.

Ethan frowned a bit at that before shrugging again.  "I guess I don't really know.  But I don't think I did. Why would I?"

Daphne wrinkled her nose.  "How should I know? I don't know you.  Were you bummed about anything? Cut from the wrestling team or failed a major test or something?"

"I play baseball," Ethan corrected, but not in an accusatory way. More like he was really proud.

Daphne rolled her eyes.  "Well, unless there's an all-stars game in Heaven, that ship has sailed."

Ethan looked demoralized at the realization that Daphne was right. "*Played* baseball," he corrected.  "But I'd been having a good season."

"So you can't think of any reason you would have killed yourself?"

Ethan shook his head.

"Any enemies?" Daphne followed up.

Ethan shook his head again. "I mean, there were school bullies and such, but I can't think of any reason someone would want me dead. That's so extreme."

Daphne respected his expression. "Yes. It's quite extreme. Why don't you walk me through the night you died? What you remember, of course."

Ethan licked his ghostly lips. "Okay." He looked nervous all of a sudden. Up until now, he'd been so casual. "I was with Jake and his girlfriend, Megan, and our other buddy, Tyler. Just a kickback at Jake's."

"What exactly were you guys doing?" Daphne asked.

"We started out playing video games." Ethan looked up, trying to remember the events of the night. "And that's about all I remember."

"So you were hanging out at your BFF's house

and then at the end of the night, fall to your death. Something obviously happened."  Daphne rolled her eyes.  "About what time were you at Jake's?"

"We had pizza for dinner."  Ethan pointed at Daphne as the memory came back into his mind.  "I often stayed to midnight, more or less, so it's possible that's the timeframe."

"And what do you remember of your death? Anything?"  Daphne crossed her ankles as she listened, trying to make some sense out of his disjointed story. How do you simply forget dying?

"I do remember walking down the street. It was dark out."  Ethan wagged a finger at Daphne as if it helped him jog his memory.  "And I saw a huge crowd of people surrounding a dead body."

"You."  It wasn't a question.

"Me."  Ethan said it so calmly and matter-of-factly, Daphne started to wonder how he could be on such an even keel about his own demise.  Someone so young should be angry at the life that was stolen.  She wasn't going to tell him that, of course, but she found it odd not to be sensing those types of negative emotions now.

"How'd you get there?"

Ethan shook his head. "I don't know how I know, but I know I was dropped there. Not pushed. Not jumped. Dropped."

Daphne nodded. She had sensed something similar already. "You were already dead by then."

"I think so."

Ethan was barely any help at all. Daphne opened her mind to see what she could sense on her own. An image flashed of a large group of kids, laughing and talking. "Could you have possibly gone to a party that night?" she probed.

"I was at the kickback at Jake's."

Daphne shook her head. "No. I'm seeing lots of kids, not just a small handful. Like a party."

Ethan tightened his lips into a straight line. "I don't remember anything about a party. I wasn't invited to any that I can think of.  I mean, that night.  I went to parties all the time."  Again, he wasn't bragging, just stating facts.

Daphne could tell everyone loved Ethan.  His death would rock his high school community.

"Any reason Jake or those people,"—she twirled a hand in the air, not having a clue of the other names because she didn't care to retain them—"would want to kill you?"

Ethan looked shocked and then disgusted, as if the whole accusation was downright heresy.  "Jake, Megan and Tyler?  No way."  He shook his head overdramatically.  "No way.  Jake was my best friend since second grade."

"But his girlfriend?  Maybe she was jealous of your friendship?  Girls can be hardcore when they're jealous."

"But murder me?  And drop me off a highway?" Ethan was still shaking his head.  "That sounds premeditated."

Daphne pouted.  She couldn't ignore that Ethan was right—it didn't sound like a jealous rage.  The flash of the party came flying back at Daphne unbidden.  She decided to probe on that a bit more.

"What kind of parties did you typically go to?" Daphne asked.

That got him to relax.  "Ya know, the baseball team was always holding huge get-togethers.  After parties, after dances and such.  The usual when parents are away. You know."

He said it again as if Daphne could relate.  She could not.  At all.  She slapped on a fake smile and powered through.  "Describe them as if I had no idea."

"Okay.  Lots of people, so packed sometimes you could barely move."  That aligned with her vision.  "Loud music.  Dancing.  Underage drinking—don't judge."

"I couldn't care less."

"People making out in various corners of the room.  Someone always doing something stupid...."

"I see a man with dark hair, surrounded by three

girls. They're laughing at something. Behind them there are lots of people packed in at what seems like a party," Daphne described.

Ethan shrugged. "I had friends with dark hair. Could be anybody, I suppose."

"So you're not really going to be much help, are you?"

Ethan shrugged. "I just don't remember leaving Jake's house."

As if on cue, Daphne's phone rang and she could see it was Miguel. Perfect timing. He could easily probe deeper on Ethan's friends and find out what party was happening the night of Ethan's death.

"We need to talk to Ethan's best friend, Jake," Daphne blurted, ignoring the usual phone-answering pleasantries.

If Miguel was caught off-guard by it, he never let it show. But the truth was, he wasn't. He loved Daphne's blunt style. "I'm stuck on desk duty."

Daphne frowned for a moment because she

preferred in-person interviews. Her psychic intuition was much keener in a face-to-face situation. She was also a consultant with the police department and not an actual officer. While she never bothered to uncover all the gritty details, she assumed the rules were slightly different for her. "I'm not. Get me an address and I'll go and then put you on speaker phone."

"Do we have a last name for Jake?" Miguel asked.

Daphne looked at Ethan and then relayed the answer. "Nova."

"Okay, give me a minute."

"And Miguel?" Daphne added. "There was a party the night of Ethan's death. I have this feeling he was there even though he says he doesn't remember it."

"And?" He knew her too well.

"Can you dig around from your desk and find out where it took place and who hosted it? I think it's an important part of this investigation."

"Of course. Thanks for giving me the easy part. You ready for Jake's address?"

She scribbled it down and hung up.  Turning to the young ghost in her living room, she said, "I need to get dressed and then you and I are going to pay a little visit to Jake's house."

"He doesn't know anything," Ethan stated again in a confident manner.

"We'll just see about that.  Now shoo!  So I can hop in the shower."

# 3.

Detective Gina Malone was one of Fresno P.D.'s finest.

In this male dominated world, she prided herself in being tough but feminine.  She always made sure to accentuate her curves and make sure her make-up was flawless.  It wasn't because of vanity.  She never wanted to have to join 'em to beat 'em.

And after ten years on the force with a record as stellar as hers, babysitting rookies was a complete insult. She silently cursed Miguel for getting shot, even though she knew it was ridiculous.  No one wanted to get shot. But if he hadn't been shot in the shoulder that one fateful night, she would be driving with Miguel, the partner whose sentences she could finish, instead of the greenie next to her.

"Are we going to talk to gangstas?" Sheffley asked like a kindergartner trying to have street cred.

Gina signaled left before turning and fought the urge to give him a death stare. Instead, she ignored him completely. So much so that in her mind, she was driving all by herself. She *wished* she was by herself. Having this rookie next to her acting this juvenile could get them both killed.

How did she end up here?

A part of her thought about lecturing Sheffley on the seriousness of their jobs and what they were about to encounter. But she wasn't his mother. Or his teacher. Or his babysitter.

He could learn the way they all had, through on-the-job training and experiences.

A few homicide cases and Sheffley wouldn't be cracking jokes about the perpetrators. Or, if he did, he'd be a complete sicko and need a psych eval. This job would wake you up fast, throw you in the deep end and leave you constantly fighting the current as you struggled to hold on to something.  Anything.  Just fighting to keep your head above water.

So she said nothing as she parked the car, barely tossing Sheffley a glance as she climbed out.  If it were Miguel, they'd have likely been tossing back theories and tactics the entire way, deciding who would ask what and take on what role.  But Miguel had respect for the job—respect for victims and their families.  Sheffley?  He was about to get a crash course in what it means to hold a badge.

There was police tape blocking off a section of sidewalk and Gina moved around it expertly.  Gina approached, Sheffley trailing behind like a puppy dog, just in time to watch the body be zipped into a bag.

Gina flashed her badge at the young man tending to the body, even though there was no need.  They all knew her.  She then asked, "Anything I need to see?"

Worldlessly, the young man unzipped the bag to

the victim's waist so Gina could see the gunshot wounds to the chest. She counted four. Young male, Hispanic. Sheffley peered around her shoulder to see for himself, and she just continued ignoring him.

The young man from the Medical Examiner's office zipped the bag back over the victim's head and said over his shoulder, "You'll have the report in a few days, but I doubt there will be any surprises."

Gina nodded. He was killed by gunshot wounds to the chest. It didn't take a medical degree to come to that conclusion. Walking away from the victim, she stormed over to the officer on the scene. Again, she flashed her badge when there really was no need. Officer Louis also knew her well.

And again, Sheffley followed her like a puppy dog, copying her movements and also showing his badge. Gina didn't introduce him or explain, so Officer Louis also ignored Sheffley and spoke directly to Gina.

"You could have come to me first, Detective Malone," Officer Louis chided her for speaking to the ME before speaking to him.

Gina rolled her eyes but didn't bother to dignify his admonishment with a response. "Give me the details."

Officer Louis pointed to a group of young men hovering near the crime scene but just outside the tape. "Vic was with his friends, walking south toward the Mini mart on the corner when a purple El Camino drove up, slowed down and shot at them."

"Purple?" It was a distinct enough color to stand out.

Officer Louis checked his notes and then nodded. "Yeah, purple. With flames apparently."

"Way to honor the art of subtlety," Gina said, shaking her head. A purple El Camino with flames should make the car easy to find, and then they'd just have to track down the owner. "Time?"

"Just after two in the a.m."

Gina pursed her lips. It was sad how long things took. The young man had been shot five hours ago and was just being removed from the scene.  So his friends had been standing there staring at their dead friend for hours.  "A big group of them and no one else was shot?"

Officer Louis pointed at one of the young men. "One was treated for a flesh wound.  Looks like he got a bullet graze, but that was it.  Apparently, it was a targeted attack.  The vic—Victor Cruz—knew his assailants."

"Oh?  That should make this an easy one, then. With a name, three witnesses and the purple El Camino, I think we could have a warrant by mid-day."

With the caseload they were handling lately, quick cases were always a welcome relief, but also Gina was thrilled to be able to wrap this case up within a day so she could part ways with Sheffley.

And she'd make sure to let The Sarge know he was no help at all.

Gina turned again and walked to where the three young witnesses, friends of Victor Cruz, were milling about. The most shocking part of seeing them was their ages.  They looked nineteen on the high end.  One of the boys still had a round face that looked to be carrying baby fat.  These were not men.  They were *boys*.  Gina hated that these kids hadn't even finished puberty and were already involved in something nobody should be involved in.

"Anyone want to tell me what happened?" Gina asked the whole group, talking to no one in particular.  She typically found that in a group of friends, there was always at least one who was willing to talk.

"It was Sharky.  He shot Victor.  We saw him do it, so go arrest him."  The young man stood taller than he was and puffed out his chest.  Gina sighed at his fake bravado.  The boy was likely an emotional wreck on the inside.

"And why would Sharky do that?" Gina asked, her hands on her hips.  She still wanted to represent authority to these kids, but she thought perhaps she could appeal to them as a mother figure.

"Ask Sharky when you find him," the young man

who'd been speaking before said again, trying to add a toughness to his shaky voice.  The other two boys never lifted their eyes from the ground in front of their feet.

"I got this," Sheffley whispered to Gina and panic set in.  But before she could process his words and stop him, Sheffley turned to the boys with a condescending tone and a loud voice.  "A detective with the Fresno Police Department is talking to you.  You want justice from us, you need to do your part and answer her!"

Gina put a hand on Sheffley's chest and tried not to laugh.  He was only a few years older than they were and getting a little too high on his horse.  "Okay, thanks Sheffley.  Let me do the interview."

Victor's friends snickered, not even bothering to hide their laughter.  The boy who had been talking to Gina before stuck out his chin and said, "Yeah, let your mom do all the work, chistoso."

They laughed again and Gina could sense the tension coming off of Sheffley.  He was going to do something stupid if she didn't de-escalate this situation immediately.  *Freaking rookies*, she thought to herself. They were handed an easy case, and he was going to complicate it with his ignorance and arrogance.

"You have no respect for the law!" Sheffley shouted and Gina shoved him back away from their witnesses.

Through gritted teeth and in what she hoped was a voice soft enough that the young boys couldn't hear, Gina whisper-yelled, "These are our witnesses.  They help us close this case quickly.  Do not get in an altercation with three teenagers who we need on our side, got it?"

Sheffley shoved her off of him and responded, "Of course.  I know what I'm doing."

"Let me do the talking.  I'm the senior detective, you're the junior.  *You* respect the law, please."  Gina was tamping down her anger, but she was just about ready to have her own partner arrested for obstruction of justice.

Sheffley gave her a dirty look but, thankfully, said nothing.  They walked back to the witnesses.

"You guys got names?" Gina asked.

"I'm Tigre, this is Gordito, and that's Mula."

Gina knew he was giving Spanish street names on purpose, but it didn't bother her.  She could get their real names easily enough when she needed them.  Tigre was the one who had been doing all the talking, so she kept the conversation going with him.

"Okay, Tigre.  Can you think of any reason Sharky would want to kill Victor?  Why did no one else get shot when the car pulled up?  Seems like even accidentally one of you should have also been a victim."

"Gordito got shot!  Show her," Tigre instructed his friend.

Gordito rolled up his sleeve and showed a thin bandage with a tiny flowering of blood seeping through. The first thought Gina had was Gordito wasn't fat enough for his nickname; he just had a round face.  Secondly, she thought this looked like the kind of fake wound she'd seen a thousand times when people wanted it to seem just real enough.

"That's not a gunshot wound, that's a papercut.

How did none of you get injured when your friend was shot multiple times?"  Gina placed her hands on her hips again.  As she spoke, she was beginning to think perhaps this wasn't as clean of a case as she'd originally thought.  Something wasn't right about this situation.

And she'd done this enough times to know to trust her intuition.

Tigre held his hands up to declare his innocence.  "Hey, we just got lucky.  Sharky only wanted to kill Victor.  I guess."

The 'I guess' was added so offhandedly that it also wasn't sitting right with Gina.  Something about their story was off.

But Sheffley just couldn't keep quiet and let her handle it.  Her skin began to burn with rage the moment she heard his voice.

"You're lying!  You'd better start telling us the full story now, you little cholo, or you'll be behind bars faster than Sharky!"

Gina barely had time to react before Tigre was up

in Sheffley's face.  "What did you call me, you racist bastard?"

"Okay, okay.  Take it down a notch."  Gina placed one hand on Tigre's chest and the other on Sheffley's and pushed them apart.  To Sheffley she overemphasized, "This is getting us nowhere."

Tigre spoke to Gina.  "You'd better control your racist little friend or this could get ugly."

Gina just really wanted to end this nightmare, so she continued the path of de-escalation.  "We're just here to help Victor get justice.  We don't want any trouble."

But Sheffley couldn't help himself and he blurted out, "Is that a threat?  Are you threatening me, pendejo?"

Gina saw the look in Tigre's eyes before she saw the gun.  He pulled a small handgun from a baggy pocket and began aiming it at Sheffley.  She couldn't deny a small part of him deserved to be punished, but this was taking the whole thing too far.

She acted purely on instinct the split-second she

saw the gun, and coincidentally it was the moment the shot rang out, reverberating through the early morning air and shattering the peace of the downtown Fresno community.

# 4.

Jake's house was fancy.  Ethan and his friends weren't from the slums.  Daphne knew that just from parking out front.  The home was large and impressive.  But the land was equally so.  The home sat back away from the street, with a large tree dominating the landscape.  There seemed to be windows everywhere, in a sleek modern style that said this home was either new or rebuilt recently.  It was definitely no tract home from 1967.

Jake Nova was a rich kid.

Daphne knew these kinds of kids, seeing as how

she'd grown up in Malibu with the children of the Hollywood elite. She didn't fit in with them, didn't like them, but she knew them.

"I don't have a badge," Daphne stated to Ethan's ghost as she climbed out of her car. "So I can't be sure how this will go. Hopefully, he'll just want to talk. For therapeutic reasons."

"Just tell him I'm here. He'll want to help me." Ethan's ghost was so confident, so eerily calm. Daphne had to push a little harder to make sure he, in fact, knew he was dead. He did. He just exuded confidence in a way so few ghosts did.

But he was delusional. "Ethan. I've been doing this for many years. Rare is the person who believes wholeheartedly and opens up completely to being told they're in the presence of a ghost. Bestie or not."

Ethan seemed to contemplate the way his friend might react. "What do they usually do?"

"Best case, they cry or get frightened. On the worst days, they throw me out as a lunatic."

Ethan cocked his head to the side before saying, "He might throw you out."

"Okay, just let me handle this. My way." Daphne shook her head at her unconventional partner. Without waiting for more retorts, she bounded up the long walkway to the large, elaborate porch.

She rang the doorbell and waited until a beautiful middle-aged woman answered the door.

"Can I help you?" the woman said in a way that meant Daphne had better make this good or she was going to get a door slammed in her face.

"Mrs. Nova? My name is Daphne Winters. I'm a consultant with the Fresno Police Department. I was hoping to speak to Jake about his friend, Ethan Bender."

Daphne could sense immediately that this woman's primary concern was protecting her son, so Daphne quickly added, "Just a formality for the case files."

Mrs. Nova's face softened slightly and she opened the door to let Daphne in as she said, "To be honest, I was sort of surprised no one has asked to talk to us yet."

Us.  This woman wasn't going to let Daphne be alone with Jake.  There was no way.

"Well, it's a pretty open and shut case and all."  Daphne decided to recite the party line.  "But we just need to get it all documented.  You know how it is.  Bureaucracy."

"Of course."  Mrs. Nova led Daphne into an impressive two-story entryway.  Daphne decided not to second-guess why this woman hadn't asked to see a badge or any kind of proof that Daphne was working with the police.  If she needed to, she could always get Miguel on the line.

"Jake!" Mrs. Nova called up the stairs without climbing even one.  "Someone's here to see you!"  And then she turned back to Daphne and said, "Sad story, really. Just awful about that poor boy.  His poor family."

But Daphne didn't need to be a psychic to see that this lady was mostly thinking, *Thank goodness it was*

*Ethan and not Jake.*  She decided to push the envelope just a little and said, "Actually, the family wants us to consider this as more than a suicide."

There.  Daphne would just let that little tidbit simmer.

But Mrs. Nova continued with fake sympathy. "Tragic.  Simply tragic."  She gestured toward a large room that looked like an open-concept family room, dining room and kitchen all in one.  The surrounding windows let in so much natural light, it created a peaceful atmosphere.  Perfect for asking a teenager about his dead friend.

"I'm honestly glad to catch Jake on a holiday.  I wasn't entirely sure he'd be home on a Monday morning."  Daphne grabbed a seat and Ethan hung out nearby.

"Well, to be honest, Jake hasn't felt like going to school since Ethan died.  But today is a teacher in-service day. That means the kids are home but the teachers have to work," Mrs. Nova explained.

It wasn't long after that when Jake Nova came trotting down the stairs.  The weight of his friend's death was plastered all across his sullen face.  His shoulders slumped and his steps were heavy-footed.

Again, Daphne didn't need any special talents to read this young man.  He was truly devastated by the loss of his best friend.  Daphne shifted in her seat, suddenly feeling uncomfortable at the prospect of interviewing him like a suspect.

As if psychically sensing her discomfort, Ethan leaned in and said, "Don't worry.  He'll cooperate.  He's on my side."

Daphne nodded at the ghost and then introduced herself when she saw the look of confusion on Jake's face.  "Hi, Jake. So sorry to disturb you this fine morning.  My name is Daphne and I'm with the Fresno Police Department.  I just wanted to hear your side of the story of what happened on the night Ethan fell to his death."  She carefully chose not to mention "interviewing" or "suicide."  "Tell me about the kickback."

Jake shrugged.  When he finally spoke, his voice was soft, injured.  He was the complete opposite of the confident ghost standing next to her.  This boy was shattered by the loss.  "Not much to tell, really.  We were all just hanging out, playing video games.  We ate some pizza. Laughed, talked. That's about it."

"And can you elaborate on what you mean by 'we'?"  Daphne could sense the young man was telling the truth and that his story aligned with Ethan's, but she wanted to ask the right questions, mostly so Mrs. Nova didn't get suspicious that this interview was more than it appeared.

Jake cleared his throat before saying, "Me, Megan, my girlfriend, Ethan and Tyler, our other friend. We hung out most weekends together."

Ethan nodded. "All true,"

"And when did the kickback come to an end?" Daphne asked.  She was trying to segue into the party scene where she knew she saw Ethan, but she had to tread lightly.

"Well, Megan and Tyler stayed until about midnight, but Ethan left around ten."

Daphne fought the urge to exchange a glance with the ghost next to her.  That was much earlier than Ethan had thought he'd left.

"I left that early?  Why?" Ethan asked.

So Daphne translated.  "Why did Ethan leave so early?"

Jake frowned.  "He didn't really say.  Just said he had to go.  I offered him a ride and he said he didn't need one.  I thought that was strange because I carted Ethan everywhere. But I didn't push it."

"Jake has a Camaro and I have nothing, so, yes, I exploited him for rides.  Sue me," Ethan said defensively next to Daphne.  She ignored him.

"You had no reason to worry about Ethan, right?" Daphne knew the truth behind the words.  Megan and Ethan had been struggling to get along, and Jake had felt the need to placate his girlfriend.  Daphne knew nothing about it from firsthand experiences, but she assumed teenage love could be more complicated than it needed to be.

"No reason at all. He walked home from my house hundreds of times since we were kids." Daphne watched Jake swallow the lump in his throat. She knew the emotion he was projecting as well as she knew her own name. It was guilt. The little rat-bastard emotion that was so overpowering and all-consuming.

If it were a tangible object, Daphne would slap it silly.

"Just to be clear, I know you had nothing to do with Ethan's death. And no reason to feel responsible in any way. I'm sure you're wondering why this would happen." Jake looked up as Daphne said the words and she knew she'd hit the mark. "And that's where I come in. I am going to get us all answers. For Ethan."

Ethan leaned in. "I think he can take it. Let him know I'm here."

Daphne resisted the urge to tell Ethan to shut up and instead just shooed him away with her hand.

Jake shook his head as he responded. "I don't know what happened to Ethan. One minute he was here with us and the next..." Jake didn't finish the sentence but he didn't need to.

Daphne leaned in. She wasn't a particularly sensitive person, but she put extra effort into making her voice sound soft and gentle. "Can you think of any reason why Ethan would want to kill himself? Would you describe him as suicidal at all when he left here?"

Jake shook his head. "No. Not at all." He spoke with great conviction. This was the crux of what he'd been struggling with. The news reports and the friend he'd known all his life were completely in contrast with one another. It simply didn't add up. "He just..."

Daphne reached to find the end of that sentence, but it was coming in fragments. Megan, Ethan, Ethan leaving... "Why did Ethan leave?"

"I mean, he and Megan might have been arguing, but they always did." Jake was pleading with Daphne. He worried that this had something to do with Ethan's death and he wished desperately that it did not.

Daphne didn't think it had anything to do with Ethan's death either, but she wanted to sense the truth in his words as he provided details. "What were they arguing about?"

Jake raised his hands like he was begging for mercy. "Nothing. Seriously. Megan wanted a turn in the game and Ethan made fun of her for it. Called her Horseface like he often did. And Megan hated that name, obviously, so she stuck up for herself. But it didn't go any further, I swear. And then Ethan got that phone call and he left, maybe fifteen minutes later."

That was it, the thing Daphne had been trying to grab onto. A phone call. "Do you know who called him?"

Jake shook his head again. "I didn't ask. He said he had to go and I told him I'd see him later. He let himself out, like he always did."

Daphne couldn't help herself and she turned to the ghost next to her. This was too important to continue the ruse in front of Jake and Mrs. Nova. "Who called you?"

She ignored Jake's horrified expression across from her.

Ethan shrugged casually, like this was no big deal. "I don't remember." He laughed. "I do remember calling Megan Horseface, though. She's such a brat. I have no idea what Jake sees in her."

Daphne snapped in front of Ethan. She didn't want to focus on Jake's ugly, bratty girlfriend. "Focus, Ethan. You went to a party after you left Jake's. We need to know who told you about it."

Mrs. Nova spoke slowly. "What type of consulting did you say you did for the Fresno Police?"

Daphne sighed. She was going to have to come clean now. "I am a psychic medium. I help them solve cases by communicating with the victim's spirits themselves."

She waited for their response, expecting Mrs. Nova at the very least to kick her out. Jake and Mrs. Nova sat there in stunned silence, so Daphne took it as a good sign that they didn't instantly shut down.  She had found there were two types of people when it came to ghosts: you either instantly put up a block, or you didn't.  So Daphne continued.  "Ethan's spirit came to me, but the trouble is he doesn't remember anything past the kickback at your house."

Mrs. Nova nodded.  "I wondered where you got the word 'kickback.'  I've never heard a grown woman say that before."

Daphne raised a brow at Mrs. Nova's logic but sensed her open-mindedness and was thankful for it.

Jake still looked shell-shocked.  "So...Ethan is here?"

Daphne nodded slowly.  She wanted to provide Jake with some healing, some peace, associated with the death of his best friend, but she didn't want to traumatize him with a ghost in the process.

"Can he prove it?" Jake asked.

Daphne scratched her nose as she thought.  Not all ghosts could move objects, especially if they weren't in a heightened state of emotion, and Ethan hadn't been emotive since she'd met him. "Ask something only you and Ethan would know."

Jake looked up at the ceiling, searching for the perfect test. But Daphne could sense the hopefulness. He *wanted* to know his friend was here. "Ask him what our nickname was for Mrs. Sutton."

Daphne scoffed. Non-psychics always assumed because they needed her to hear the ghosts, that it worked the same in reverse. "He can hear you."

But next to her, Ethan just laughed again. This boy sure did enjoy his afterlife. "We called her Mrs. Buttersworth. You know? Like the fat lady on the syrup?"

"Classy," Daphne muttered toward Ethan, but to Jake she responded, "Mrs. Buttersworth, after the syrup."

Jake's face lit up at the realization that Ethan was, in fact, in the room. But Mrs. Nova turned to her son and asked, "Why on Earth would you call her that?"

Jake just shrugged and Daphne stayed silent. She

wasn't going to out the boys that it was in reference to her overweight body type.  Let her wonder if maybe it had something to do with her sticky sweet personality.

"So he's here?  He's really here?" Jake asked, a smile creeping across his face for the first time.

"Yes, he's here.  And now you know why I am so desperate to know who called him.  Ethan went somewhere after he left your house and before he died."

Jake lifted an eyebrow.  "Can't you just have the cops pull the phone records?"

Daphne smiled.  She was so useless at "manual methods."  But it *would* give Miguel something to do while he was stuck on desk duty.  "Yes.  I believe we can." Daphne stood.  "Thank you for your time.  You've been very helpful."

"You said he went to a party?" Jake asked.

"Yes.  Well, he doesn't remember it, but I see flashes of a scene with lots of kids dancing and Ethan is definitely there.  I believe he went to a party after he left your house, yes."  Daphne crossed her arms as she waited for whatever hung in the balance of Jake's mind.

"There *was* a party that night.  It was at Arianna's house."  Jake looked at his hands as he remembered the details, any details that might help clear his friend's name from the accusation of suicide.  "We had all thought it was going to be lame, so we decided not to go and hung out here instead."

"Why would it be lame?  Were you guys nerds or something?"  Daphne knew the answer to that, but she needed to prod Jake.

Jake huffed at the ridiculous accusation.  "Nah. It's 'cause Arianna has been obsessed with Ethan since the fifth grade.  We always tried to avoid her.  For Ethan's sake.  She's nothing but trouble."

Daphne looked at Ethan.

He shrugged and said, "What can I say?  The girl was off her rocker.  But she couldn't resist me."

"Did you go to Arianna's party?" Daphne asked, no trace of humor in her tone since she felt she knew the answer already.

"I don't know why I would," was all Ethan could say.

So Daphne turned to Jake. "Does Arianna have a last name?"

"Of course. It's Puente."

"I guess I know who I'm talking to next," Daphne said to no one in particular. To Jake and Mrs. Nova she said, "Thank you for your time." She turned to let herself out.

"Wait!" Jake stood up. Daphne turned back around as Jake continued. "Can you tell Ethan something for me? Tell him... Tell him he's the best friend I ever had. And I wish... I wish I'd never let him go that night. If I could go back in time, he would've spent the night at my house. Tell him. Tell him Bros till the end. No. Bros for *eternity*."

Daphne smiled as she felt the pain in Jake's chest ease just a bit. She had been so focused on solving Ethan's mystery, she had forgotten momentarily about the healing that others might need. This was the reason she loved doing what she did.  She loved giving Jake a chance to share his final thoughts with someone he'd loved and lost.  She loved ensuring he knew for a certain fact that he was getting the chance to say goodbye to his best friend.

Something he thought he'd never get to do.

She was still smiling as she simply said yet again, "He can hear you."

# 5.

"Well, that was a shitshow."  Gina flopped in her seat across from Miguel in the bullpen.

Without looking up, Miguel asked, "What happened?"

Gina crumpled a piece of paper from her desk and used it as a softball to pitch it toward Miguel's head. "Thanks for getting shot, asshole."

This time Miguel looked up.  "What happened? Sheffley not ready yet?"  He could picture the challenge of taking on a newbie.  It was a lot harder than it seemed.

Gina made a gagging sound.  "He'll never be ready.  Some people just don't have the right instincts, ya know?"

Miguel nodded.  He knew it as well as Gina did. This time he laughed at her as he asked, yet again, "What exactly happened?"

"He decided to get into an altercation with my witness.  And, yes, in case you're wondering, he called them cholos."

Miguel frowned a bit, knowing full well as a Latino man how that word would be received.  Miguel himself believed that if you don't want to be perceived in a certain way, you shouldn't dress the part.  It was why he always dressed impeccably, with not a hair out of place. People judged by looks. Didn't make it all right to derail an investigation because of your prejudice.  "I take it the witnesses didn't appreciate it?"

Gina shook her head as she said, "Pulled a gun."

Miguel was actually shocked.  "What?"

"Look.  The whole thing was shady from the get-go.  A drive-by shooting where no one else gets shot but the vic, apparently some vendetta against the guy. You know how hard it is to pull something like that off in a moving vehicle.  But the so-called friends he was with? They knew something.  I think they may have even been in on it."

Miguel was listening intently.

He knew they didn't have time to chase down accessories to a murder that could be easily solved with less collateral, but he also knew Gina's instincts were on point.  "So you were trying to get them to fess up when Sheffley opened his big mouth?"

"Basically.  I told him let me do the talking.  But could he listen?"

"Did anyone get hurt?  I mean from Sheffley's nonsense."  Miguel knew he had to clarify, since obviously Gina had been there in the first place because someone was dead.

The manic energy seemed to deflate out of Gina. Telling the story was cathartic.  "No.  I was able to push the gun toward the ground before it went off and then get the gun from his hands before Tigre could shoot it again.  He's in a holding cell and Sheffley is talking to

Internal Affairs.  Per protocol we had to report the incident."

"And meanwhile the perp rides around Fresno with not a care in the world."  Miguel shook his head at Sheffley's short-sightedness.

Gina sighed.  "Not for long, I'm sure.  His name is Sharky and he shot Cruz from a purple El Camino. Shouldn't be too hard to track him down."

"Good.  Wrap that one up and help me with the Ethan Bender case."  Miguel shifted in his seat to face Gina as he caught her up to speed.  "Daphne spoke to Ethan's best friend and got a potential name for where he went that night."

"Daphne?  Talking to witnesses on her own now?"  Gina raised an eyebrow at the lack of procedural.

Miguel gave Gina a look.  "Who's going to stop her?"

"Fair point."  Gina leaned back in her chair.  "But is this really the best use of our time?"  To emphasize her point, she lifted a pile of folders from her desk and shook them in his face. "Teenagers commit suicide. And we have dozens of actual murders to solve."

Miguel shook his head. "Daphne says he didn't commit suicide."

"Allegedly."

"You know she's right."

Gina groaned. "I know. But I don't want her to be right." Still slouched in her chair, Gina locked eyes with Miguel. "All right, fill me in. Anything has to be better than going to another crime scene with Sheffley."

"So, Ethan was at his best friend's house playing video games. He left around ten p.m., which was earlier than usual according to this friend." Miguel leaned toward Gina conspiratorially. "Get this. He got a phone call just before he left and Daphne senses that he went to a party."

"Okay? But what does Ethan say? And why does a party equal murder?" Gina crossed her arms.

"Apparently, Ethan doesn't remember that night." Miguel frowned mulling over the meager evidence.  "And I don't know where the murder comes in, but…"  He shuffled papers around his desk until he grabbed the one he wanted.  "But I pulled the phone records and he didn't just get one call when he was at his friend's house.  He got tons.  From the same number."

Gina stood up to peer over Miguel's shoulder at the phone log.  She scanned and counted more than twenty easily.  "Okay.  So someone really wanted him at that party.  Whose number is that?"

"Another classmate of Ethan's named Jalen Puente."  Miguel looked up at Gina as he explained, "According to Daphne, who asked Ethan, this guy wasn't a friend of Ethan's."

Gina leaned back and rested a hand on the back of Miguel's chair.  "Then why did he want to get hold of Ethan so badly?"

"The very night Ethan ends up dead."  Miguel turned back to the paper in his hand.  "And I checked.  No other calls from Jalen before that night around ten p.m., and no other calls after Ethan leaves Jake's house."

Gina pursed her lips as she turned over everything Miguel was telling her in her mind. "Okay. I'm intrigued, Detective Alvarez. Are we on our way to talk to this Jalen Puente?"

Miguel looked like a battered man as he stared at the ground and said, "I can't. Desk duty, remember? Daphne is on her way there now."

Gina knelt down to be closer to Miguel's seated level. "First of all, we were just on our way to lunch. You can take a lunch break, right? Secondly, I'm pretty sure Daphne isn't allowed to interview witnesses without us, so we're already breaking the rules." Gina moved to grab the keys from her desk. "And you're not Sheffley, so I highly doubt there will be anything physical to injure you. We're just asking a few questions."

Miguel smiled at Gina's logic.

He hated breaking the rules—it went against everything he believed in. But he was really curious about this case, and he couldn't just sit at his desk making calls all day while Gina and Daphne did all the work.

"Yeah. Let's just go to lunch. Surely, we can do that." He spoke louder than he needed to so anyone listening in would think that was where he was headed.

"And it just so happens our lunch date includes a witness." Gina shrugged. "It happens."

Miguel laughed as he stood. "It's never happened in the history of my career."

Gina slapped his back, careful to avoid his still-healing wounded shoulder. "There's a first time for everything, my friend."

"I'll call Daphne and let her know we'll meet her there."

"You know I adore your little freaky girlfriend, but her laissez-faire attitude is going to get you in hot water one day." Gina shook her head, but she was smiling the entire time.

She had taken to Daphne's methods faster than Miguel had.

Miguel smiled and the tenderness in his eyes told Gina exactly how he felt about the blonde psychic.

"There's no one else like her on this planet, that's for sure," he said sincerely.

# 6.

Daphne was in front of the Puente family home, leaning against her car, when Gina and Miguel pulled up and parked behind her.

Miguel and Gina were barely out of the car when Daphne blurted, "This is where the party was." She gestured with her chin toward the house behind them. It was a simple home, nothing extravagant. The flower beds were lined with brightly colored, cheerful flowers. The white paint was clean. Garage door was closed. Nothing littered the lawn or the driveway. The house was small, but it looked loved and well cared for.

Miguel nodded to acknowledge her statement and then surprised Daphne by pulling her into an embrace.  He whispered in her ear, "Is Ethan here?"

Daphne pulled away and stared at Miguel's handsome face.  "Are ghosts secrets now?  He's been with me all day."

It wasn't really something he needed to hide from Gina. It just felt more natural for Miguel to be discreet when solving murder cases with ghosts and mediums.  Of course, the opposite was completely true with Daphne, so she just rolled her eyes at Miguel's behavior.

One day, he'd be more comfortable with ghosts. To be with Daphne meant spirits were a daily part of your life. The more he was around her, the more Miguel was going to get used to it.

Gina ignored the whole interchange, remaining focused on getting caught up to speed.  "Miguel's on lunch so we need to get down to business.  Jalen called Ethan like twenty times that night, so he really wanted him at this party.  Is that what we're after?  Do we think he ambushed him or something?"

Daphne stared at the house and used her intuition to get an honest answer for Gina. "No, I don't think it was an ambush. Jalen's sister, Arianna, has apparently been infatuated with Ethan for years."

Gina and Miguel exchanged a look. Then Miguel turned to Daphne to explain. "Infatuation, obsession, stalking, murder. Not always mutually exclusive."

Daphne frowned and chewed her lip as she thought about it. "I'm not getting any murderer vibes here."

"Then let's just see if we can get some details on what happened at that party." Miguel gestured for the two women to lead the way. And they did, right up to the large, imposing front door.

"These are high school students, right? Are we sure they don't have school today?" Gina asked, just now realizing that the very people they were coming to talk to might not even be home.

"Something about an in-service." Daphne spoke the foreign words, having no clue what they meant. "The kids are home today."

Daphne used the door knocker to slam three loud knocks to announce their arrival, but when Mrs. Puente answered the door, Gina stopped Daphne from speaking. This needed to be a police investigation with a psychic consultant, and not the other way around.

"Is this the Puente residence?" Gina asked.

The woman smiled cordially, but there was no warmth. She looked skittish and skeptical of the reason for three strangers on her doorstep. "Yes, it is. How can I help you?"

Gina flashed her badge. "Fresno P.D., homicide division, ma'am. Just need to speak to Jalen and Arianna Puente. Are they your children?"

Gina was so serious in her official tone that even Daphne stood still and quiet beside her. She was so commanding, Daphne had to admire her.

But those words had the intended effect, and Mrs. Puente changed her stance immediately to one on heightened alarm. She had the body language of someone one heartbeat from fight-or-flight mode. "Yes, those are my kids. What is this about? A homicide?"

"You are aware that a young man who goes to school with Arianna and Jalen was killed a few days ago? A young man named Ethan Bender?" Gina stuck her chin out, challenging this woman to deny it.

"Well, I know a classmate committed suicide, but it has nothing do with us." Mrs. Puente stepped outside her home, closing the front door behind her.

Miguel jumped in. "We are under the impression that there was a party here at your home last weekend, and that was possibly the last time Ethan Bender was seen alive. We just need to ask your kids a few questions and we'll be out of your way."

Mrs. Puente blinked a few times to clear her head. "A party? No, no, no. They just had a few friends over. I'm sure it has nothing to do with the young man's death."

"Mrs. Puente, your son Jalen called Ethan multiple times that night. I've pulled the phone records.

If not the last person to see him alive, he was certainly one of the last people to speak to him on the phone." Miguel put his hands on his hips, exposing his own badge in the process. "So, we're going to need to speak with Jalen and Arianna now, please."

Mrs. Puente was clearly flustered, but she eventually acquiesced and led the investigators inside. Daphne didn't blame her. Miguel and Gina were intimidating, and Daphne knew this mother was completely ignorant. Not having any kids herself, Daphne wondered how many parents truly knew what their teenagers were up to.

As Mrs. Puente went to get her kids, Daphne leaned into Miguel and said, "She's telling the truth. She really didn't know her kids had thrown a party. I think she thinks she gave birth to Jesus and the Virgin Mary." Daphne completed her statement with a roll of her eyes.

Miguel squeezed Daphne's hand. "Well, glad to know it's not because she's an accessory."

The two teenagers that walked into the room

were nervous, curled in on themselves like they wanted to form a cocoon they could hide in. Daphne noticed they did not have the overwhelming sadness that Jake had. They were worried. Hiding something. She was instantly on alert for whatever came out of their mouths.

"Arianna? Jalen?" Gina asked, and continued when they nodded in affirmation. "This will just be a minute."

Miguel and Gina sat, making themselves comfortable. Luring them, Daphne assumed. Miguel gestured for the kids to do the same, and they complied, but Mrs. Puente remained standing, as did Daphne.

Miguel cleared his throat and then asked, "Can you tell us about the get-together you had this past weekend?"

Arianna looked at her brother with wide eyes, but it was clear she wanted him to do all the talking. Daphne watched them closely.

Jalen answered, "We just had a few friends over. Nothing big."

"And how late did they stay?" Miguel pulled out a notebook from his front pocket and began writing.

Jalen looked at Arianna before shrugging. Mrs. Puente hit the back of her son's head and said, "Answer the man. With words. You don't shrug to a police officer."

Miguel nodded a thanks to the mother and then waited for Jalen to respond.

"I don't know, maybe midnight?"

"And were you both here that night? For the party?" Miguel gestured between the brother and sister. They nodded but didn't elaborate. "And was Ethan Bender here at the party?"

Jalen and Arianna exchanged a look, and Daphne could see the fear on Arianna's face as strongly as she felt it flooding the room. Jalen then turned to Miguel and said, "Yeah. He was here for a bit."

Daphne chanced it and spared a glance at Ethan, who was watching the whole thing from a corner of the room. His arms were folded across his chest and his face gave nothing away.

"So, you all were good friends?" Miguel asked.

"Not really," Jalen muttered.

"So, you had a few friends over but decided to invite someone who wasn't really your friend?"  Miguel raised a brow skeptically.  Mrs. Puente leaned in, curious about where this was all heading and nervous about how much trouble her kids were in.

"He just showed up."  Jalen spoke quickly, too quickly.

This time it was Gina who jumped in.  "We have the phone records.  You called Ethan Bender more than twenty times the night he died, and after those calls, he came to *your* party.  And then he died. Care to explain?"

She didn't change her posture or raise her voice, but Gina let that little grenade drop in the room and sat there, waiting to see who jumped on it before it exploded.

"It's not like that."  Jalen stood up, a bead of sweat forming on his upper lip, and it wasn't just from the Fresno heat.

"We're listening," Miguel said, speaking calmly, matching Gina's professional demeanor.

Jalen looked back at Arianna again. Daphne could sense that he was torn between protecting himself and his sister. The dam was about to burst and Arianna would be thrown straight into the rush of roaring water.

And while they were having their little brother and sister interchange, Ethan announced, "I remember something." Daphne wanted to acknowledge Ethan, encourage him to give her the details, but without coming across as crazy to the Puentes, who were clearly having a moment of their own. So she nodded at Ethan and gave him a small thumbs up she hoped no one else noticed.

"It wasn't a party!" Ethan was laughing, almost uncontrollably. Daphne had to fight the urge to tell him to stop acting like a lunatic. "Jalen was dealing drugs. He's a drug dealer."

Ethan was still laughing as everything clicked into

place for Daphne.  The brother and sister duo weren't worried about Ethan.  They just didn't want to get busted for their side hustle.  But there was something there with Arianna.  She was being far too quiet.  And she was the link to Ethan.  Daphne reached, dug, climbed, letting her intuition be her guide.

"I got it!" Daphne blurted, clapping her hands as she did.  If she had wanted to appear sane, she'd annihilated that wish.  Everyone in the room was looking at her like she was from another planet.  "Arianna was the mastermind all along."

# 7.

Arianna shot straight up, standing to match her brother, a look of shock—mixed with a twinge of guilt—plastered across her face.

"I had nothing to do with whatever happened to Ethan."  Arianna was careful not to mention his death explicitly. "He was my friend."

This time Mrs. Puente jumped in.  "What exactly do you mean by 'mastermind'?  Is Arianna being accused of something?"

Hesitant to confirm or deny, Gina and Miguel just looked at Daphne.  Gina looked more than mildly annoyed.

"Jalen was—" Daphne struggled to find the right

word that would help Ethan's case without leading them down a rabbit hole about the drug-dealing. "—working for Arianna. The business. The get-together. Calling Ethan over. It was all Arianna's idea and planning."

Arianna opened her mouth and then closed it. Jalen looked shocked but said nothing.

Mrs. Puente stood up next to her children, an arm around Arianna. "What are you talking about?"

Daphne stared at Jalen, debating how much to divulge here and now. She gave him a condescending look, trying to urge him to out himself. "This was no ordinary get-together happening here that night, was it, Jalen?"

Jalen simply shrugged and looked away. Mrs. Puente watched the whole thing wide-eyed. She clearly wanted answers. She was absolutely in the dark about everything her children were up to.

"Arianna." Daphne turned her missiles to the leader of the operation. "Care to explain to the group why you needed Ethan here so badly that night?"

Arianna swallowed hard but said nothing.

"She liked me, obviously," Ethan explained.  "But it was more than that.  She wanted me to help her sell drugs to the athletes."

"Were you trying to recruit him?" Daphne asked.

"Daphne, can you just fill us all in on what you're sensing?" Miguel asked gently.  He didn't relish not being in on the line of questioning.

Daphne put her hands on her hips and continued talking to the teenage brother and sister.  "Are you going to tell everyone?  Or shall I?"

When Arianna and Jalen both looked at the ground, it was clear they weren't talking.  In fact, Daphne knew they were planning to lie and deny everything the minute she explained it.

"They're drug dealers and they wanted Ethan to help them with distribution."  Daphne stared them down, daring them to deny it.

But Mrs. Puente reacted before they could open their mouths to lie.  "What?  In my house?  This better be a big misunderstanding."

"Of course not, Mom," Arianna said defensively, but her glance at Daphne said far more than it should, to everyone—whether they were psychic or not.

"Daphne is a psychic medium who helps the Police Department solve cases.  She has her own methods for knowing the truth, so I'm inclined to believe her," Miguel explained, calmly and rationally.  He was so put-together in his suit and slicked-back hair, he was hard not to trust.  He gave Daphne a credibility she could never give herself, sitting there with her platinum-blonde hair sticking up in every direction.

Mrs. Puente gave her daughter a death-stare and then turned to Daphne.  "So you have a *feeling* that my children are drug dealers.  That's quite the accusation.  There had better be more proof than your psychic powers."

"Well, in this case, I could sense it was the truth, but no, it wasn't a feeling.  I got the information from Ethan himself.  He's been with me since he died."

Daphne couldn't help but smirk as she watched Arianna squirm.

"Arianna has always been a bit weird, but essentially harmless," Ethan told Daphne. "She kind of got mixed up with the wrong crowd and has had a tough couple of years. I never wanted to date her, but I never had any bad feelings about her or anything. I hope she gets her life back on track."

"He just told me, Arianna, that you're a good person who got mixed up with bad people. He still wants you to change back to the person he knew growing up," Daphne translated to the living.

Arianna swallowed and took a deep breath before asking, "He did?"

Daphne nodded, a little gentleness rubbing off on her at Ethan's forgiveness. "He did. So, do you want to fill us in on what exactly took place while he was here at your little drug-dealing get-together? Or shall I have Ethan tell his side first?"

She was bluffing, of course, since Ethan's details

were murky at best, but Arianna and Jalen didn't know that.

Arianna looked at Jalen and he shrugged. He was the older brother but clearly not the brains of the operation. He took all his cues from his younger sister. And either they really believed Daphne, or they just knew the jig was up.

Arianna sighed. "Well, there really isn't that much to tell. Yes, we called Ethan over that night. I'd wanted him to help us for a while. You know, he's popular." She shrugged, as if that said it all. "He can easily move in circles where I don't. He was here for a bit, heard us out, and then left. Honestly, that's the whole story."

"When you say, 'for a bit,' how long would you say that was?" Gina jumped back in with the questioning now that she and Miguel knew all the other pieces.

Arianna frowned. "I don't know, maybe an hour? He was gone before midnight, for sure." She looked to her brother for corroboration and he nodded emphatically.

"And while he was here, did you witness any altercation or disagreement Ethan had with any of your other…guests?" Miguel asked.

"Everyone here was from our high school and they all loved Ethan.  Everyone did," Arianna explained.

"And what did Ethan answer?  To your proposal?" Gina asked Arianna, although she spared a glance at Daphne.

Arianna looked at the ground, the guilt of it all crashing down around her.  "He wasn't interested.  He told me—"  She looked up at Daphne.  "—that I was better than all this."

"That sounds like him," Daphne responded.

"So this is all true?"  Mrs. Puente was so in shock that she was still a few minutes behind in the conversation.  "You tried to get a dead boy to help you sell drugs?  What world am I living in?"

"He was fine when he left here."  Jalen turned toward the detectives.  "Honest."

"When he left, he was on foot?  He just walked out the front door?" Gina asked.

"No."  Jalen looked confused, as if everyone should know this.  "His girlfriend picked him up."

Miguel and Gina exchanged a glance as Ethan whispered to Daphne, "I have a girlfriend?"

"Do you have a name for this girlfriend?" Gina asked as follow-up.

"Ummm… Taylor?  Theresa?  Some T name.  He waited here for about fifteen minutes after calling her and then she picked him up.  We don't know where he went after that."

Daphne looked at Ethan and spared no pretenses for the non-psychics in the room when she asked, "T name ringing a bell?"

Ethan rubbed his chin as he thought.  The whole room seemed to press pause as they waited for Daphne to get answers from the world of spirits.

Slowly, Ethan said, "Well.  I did know someone named Tyra.  But I don't think she was my girlfriend."

"Tyra," Daphne translated for the room.

"I think that's it. Tyra," Jalen confirmed.

"Then I guess that's where we go next." Miguel stood up and Gina followed.

"So if my kids stop with the drugs, they're off the hook?" Mrs. Puente asked, hope overflowing in her eyes.

"Oh, we can't say that. It's just not our case. They're young, first offense, the prosecutor might take it easy on you guys. But I hope you've learned a valuable lesson." Miguel gave the teenagers that look all holier-than-thou adults give kids they think should be better than they are.

When they were outside, Daphne felt the need to tell Miguel, "She hasn't learned her lesson, you know. Arianna. She's a troublemaker with a capital T. If it's not drugs, it will be something else. It's just who she is. Hopefully, her brother can escape her antics though. There's hope for that guy."

Miguel grimaced. "What a lovely sentiment, Daphne. Thank you for destroying my hope in the future."

"Nah, not the whole future.  Just hers."

"Okay, let's have the last name so we can go talk to Tyra before Miguel's lunch hour comes to an end," Gina instructed.

"Oh, he doesn't know it.  And she's not his girlfriend," Daphne explained.

"How does this guy know nothing about his own life?" Miguel asked.

"Excuse me.  It's his death he knows nothing about," Daphne clarified.

"Did she go to his high school?  How does he know her and how can we find her?" Gina asked.

Daphne turned to Ethan's ghost.  "Okay, Ethan. You heard the detective.  Give us something to go on."

"Tyra is Jake's older cousin.  A college girl."  Ethan nodded his head triumphantly.

Daphne just rolled her eyes.  "So what was Jake's older cousin doing picking you up at eleven p.m. the night you were murdered?"

Ethan frowned. "I don't know."

"Did she typically give you rides places?" Daphne asked.

Ethan shook his head. "No. I only saw her a few times at Jake's house. I mean, we flirted a lot, but that's about it."

Daphne turned to Miguel. "It's definitely suspicious. She's Jake's cousin but Ethan barely knew her. Why was she picking him up from a drug dealer's house?"

Miguel turned to Gina. "And was she the last person to see Ethan Bender alive?"

# 8.

"Ah, crap," Gina groaned as she looked at her phone. "I have to give a statement to IA about Sheffley's little snafu this morning." She shook her head as she put her phone back in her pocket. "Is it just me, or do the recruits get worse and worse every year?"

Miguel just laughed. "Go. Give your statement. I'll ride to Tyra's with Daphne and we'll fill you in later."

"All right. Although, I have to say I'm a little bummed. From a straightforward suicide to drug-dealing teenagers and a shady late-night rendezvous, this case is getting juicier and juicier by the minute."

"Okay, got the address and a last name from Jake." Daphne shook her phone as emphasis of the non-psychic methods she used to help the investigation. "He also confirmed that Ethan didn't know Tyra very well and he found it hard to believe he would ask her for a ride in the middle of the night."

"Then we definitely need to hear the story from Tyra's point of view," Miguel confirmed. "Let's go." He moved to climb in Daphne's car but spoke to Gina as he walked. "Call me as soon as you're done and we can meet up."

"Okay. And Miguel?" Gina held her door open and waited for Miguel's attention. "Be back at HQ by one so no one starts to wonder. I don't want to be giving a statement about *you* to Internal Affairs any time soon."

Miguel acknowledged his tight timeframe and then Gina drove back in blissful silence. Two bizarre cases that were not all what they appeared to beon the surface, and all before noon on a Monday.

And she hated to admit it, but without Daphne

they wouldn't even have investigated much about Ethan Bender.  Sure, the family had questions and nothing *was* adding up, but with all the cases needing attention, a teenage suicide just wouldn't have been the highest priority for resource-constrained detectives.

But it was clear now that they were on to something.

Gina walked into the building downtown made almost entirely of glass.  It was a beautiful place to work, even if it could get really hot letting in that Central Valley sun in the summertime.  She whistled quietly to herself as she headed to the IA office.  She couldn't wait to see what punishment Sheffley had gotten for being so careless with a witness they needed.

But she had barely passed her desk when Spencer, their tech wizard, called her name.  She figured a short conversation with him wouldn't get her in any trouble, so she met him halfway.

"What's up?"

"I found that car.  The purple El Camino.  If this is

their getaway car, then they aren't very bright.  They're pretty proud of it.  Everything is registered openly, paid annually.  And get this—they enter it in car shows and such all around the state."  To accentuate his words, Spencer handed a stack of documents supporting everything he had told Gina.

"Hmmmm.  Frank and Mona Alecante.  Judging by date of birth, they're in their fifties.  I highly doubt they were driving during a drive-by murder."  Gina looked up at Spencer, smiling broadly.  "Great work, Spence."

"Anytime."  Spencer grinned.  He saluted Gina and walked back to his desk.  Gina continued on to the IA office she'd been summoned to.

Abigail Whitehurst sat at her desk, scrutinizing Gina as she walked in.  Gina was confident in what she knew and surprisingly eager to tattle on Sheffley, so she sat down, not at all nervous.  Abigail sat across from her, hair pulled back tight, lips pursed, her face a brick wall revealing nothing.

"Care to fill me in on why you provoked a

situation to the point of Detective Sheffley almost getting shot?"  Abigail jumped right in, and Gina froze.  He had spun the entire story around.  Gina should've been prepared for that, but she hadn't been, and this epiphany caught her off guard.

"What?  That's not what happened at all."  Driven by shock, Gina knew she sounded like an idiot.  She willed herself to calm down and handle this professionally.

"According to the statements I have from multiple witnesses, you prevented Sheffley from doing his job, failed to de-escalate a situation with a criminal, and then allowed that criminal to pull a weapon and fire on your partner.  So, please, enlighten me on what you feel actually happened."  Abigail leaned back in her chair, her face a hard rock of jagged lines and harsh edges.

"That wasn't a criminal.  He was a witness.  In my attempt to interview said witness, Sheffley kept escalating the situation with taunts and derailing my investigation."  Gina felt her voice rising and she swallowed to try and get herself back under control.  If she came across as emotional it could discount everything she was saying.  And Sheffley was the bad guy here, not Gina.  "When Sheffley called my witness a cholo, which I assure you was racially motivated and not relevant in any way to the work we were doing, the witness got angry and tried to shoot Sheffley.  If I hadn't been there, Sheffley would be in the hospital right now."

"The officer on the scene..."  Abigail consulted her notes before stating, "an Officer Louis, has corroborated Sheffley's story completely.  He said you broke protocol multiple times, starting with not consulting with him the minute you got there to get debriefed.  And then you tried to exclude your partner from doing his job, all of which led to the altercation."

"Have you spoken to the witness?  He's in County Jail right now.  Ask him why he pulled a gun on Sheffley.  It had nothing to do with me.  That much I know."

"I can look into that," which was code for probably-not-going-to-waste-my-time-on-that.  "At this point, I have no choice but to recommend disciplinary action."

"And what about Sheffley?"  Gina couldn't believe her ears.  If she got in trouble and he didn't...the very thought at such injustice had her fuming.

"His situation is not your concern.  But honestly, it seems to me that you never gave him a chance to screw up.  You kept blocking him from doing his job.  So maybe next time let someone screw up before you decide they're not good enough for you."  Abigail gestured to the door.  "That'll be all."

"This is ridiculous.  I didn't do anything wrong."  Gina chastised herself for how whiny she was coming across.

Abigail just pointed again at her door.  "I said, that will be all."

Gina was in a complete daze as she wandered down the hallway back to her desk. Were she and Miguel both about to be sidelined with two cases that needed to be solved?

She tried to focus on the work, thought about

next steps with Frank and Mona Alecante, but she simply couldn't move past her conversation—no, sabotage—with Abigail Whitehurst in cahoots with newbie-detective Sheffley and sensitive-egoed Officer Louis.

She threw the papers Spencer had given her on her desk, but it wasn't satisfying enough, so she picked up a couple of pens and threw them at her monitor screen. Over a decade on the force and her record was impeccable. Until now.

Thanks to that imbecile.

She had to stop herself from hunting him down and having a confrontation right here in front of everyone. But she knew that would only make things worse, and more than anything what she wanted to do was join Daphne and Miguel in interviewing witnesses and solving cases.

So she decided not to just sit there waiting for the guillotine to fall. She would take matters into her own hands.

Standing up and smoothing out her clothes, she

took deep soothing breaths so she wouldn't come across as an emotional basket case.  And then she marched head-on right into The Sarge's glass-walled office, closing the door behind her.  She did *not* need the entire bullpen to know Sheffley had gotten the better of her.

"The whole thing is bullshit," Gina announced.

The Sarge raised an eyebrow and leaned back in his seat, hands folded across his lap.  "Is it?"

"Sheffley provoked a witness which led to a violent altercation where someone could have been seriously hurt.  And that drive-by?  It's not as clear cut as it first appeared. We have work to do and he lost us precious time with his outburst."  There.  She laid it out as plainly as she could.

The Sarge just sighed.  "Sit down, Malone."

She was used to a boisterous, overbearing man. A grizzly with a temper.  This man who looked so disappointed in her as he spoke calmly and resolvedly? He scared her a little bit.

She sat quietly.

"Sheffley's as green as a baby twig.  You don't think I know that?  I could've paired him up with any two-bit asshole detective I've got.  I chose you so you could train him.  Make him useful to all of us.  You tired of a never-ending caseload?"  When Gina nodded, The Sarge continued, still speaking calmly.  Too calmly.  "Yeah. We all are.  I had to *fight* to get us more people, and you screw all that up the very first day?  I trusted you, Gina."

Gina felt herself shrinking back into the seat, feeling smaller and smaller with every word.  She wished he would yell, throw things, be the man she was used to.  The guy breaking everything down for her with respect and kindness was unnerving at best.

Gina *had* screwed up.

"I...I didn't realize."  Gina barely recognized her own tiny voice.

"Well, I think you'll find that the punishment fits the crime.  Sheffley is your new partner.  And from now on, his record is your record, understood?  He so much as pisses on the wrong bush and it's you who'll pay for it."

Gina nodded.  She wanted to scream, to beg for anything but that, but she knew it was fruitless.  Maybe a small part of her did deserve this.  She asked, "What about Miguel?"

"Don't you worry about Alvarez.  I have plenty he can do from his desk, and when he's back one-hundred percent, we'll see how partners land.  For now, you and Sheffley go find me the drive-by shooter so we can get more little shits off the street.  Please."

Gina stood, but she wasn't quite ready to leave. She wanted to apologize, take some responsibility for letting her boss down.  But she couldn't find the words. So she simply said, "Sheffley will be a star detective by the end of the year."

"I hope so, Malone."  The Sarge pointed at her. "For your sake."

Gina couldn't help the giant exhale that escaped her lips when she made it back to her desk in the bullpen. She then picked up her phone and cradled it in her hands.

She had no idea how this had all gotten so out of

control.  She had no idea how she had been so dismissive of Sheffley when she knew they needed help.  She had to be honest about the fact that she'd been having a bit of a tantrum at the prospect of training someone.  And she was really not excited about working with Sheffley instead of Miguel.  This was going to be a waking nightmare.

And worst of all, she had no idea how she was going to break this awful news to Miguel.

# 9.

"Wow.  That's quite the house," Miguel stated as Daphne parked the car in front of a large, brick home.  It had a classic feel to it which completely exuded wealth and economic status.

"Yeah.  Jake's house wasn't exactly the slums either.  This family is well to-do," Daphne explained to Miguel.

Miguel turned to Daphne.  "Are you getting anything?"

Daphne looked at the house and opened up her senses. "Nothing serious.  This is a good family; Tyra is a good girl.  Her family has high expectations for her." Daphne shrugged.  "There's no nefarious vibes like there were with Arianna, that's for sure."

"All right.  Let's go find out what she knows then."  Miguel climbed out of the car.  "And I hope she cuts to the chase because my 'lunch hour' is running out."

"Got any theories, Ethan?" Daphne asked the ghost as they approached the brick mansion.

"Nope.  I'm as curious as you all.  If I could call anyone for a ride, I have no idea why I'd call her.  Why wouldn't I call Jake?" Ethan shrugged.

"He's clueless," Daphne explained to Miguel.

Miguel shook his head.  "Seriously. How does a ghost know so little about his last day on the planet?  This would go much faster if he could remember."

Daphne rolled her eyes.  "Oh, excuse him.  Is the murder victim not cooperating properly with your investigation, Detective?"

"Ugh, Daphne.  No, that's not what I meant." Miguel sighed.  "I just don't understand how he could not remember his own murder."

"If it was your last day on earth, would you choose to focus on the good times? Or all the things that weren't so great? Ethan is just choosing to focus on the positive. Hanging out with friends? A highlight of his last day. Hanging out with drug dealers and then meeting an untimely demise? Not a highlight."

"I guess so," Miguel muttered.

Ethan whispered "thanks" to Daphne and she responded with a wink. Living people were sometimes enigmas, but ghosts? Ghosts she could read like a book.

"There is one thing that does have me baffled about Ethan, though." Daphne spoke slowly, not sure how to voice what was nagging at her senses. Both Miguel and Ethan stared at her, waiting for her explanation. "He's pretty nonchalant about the whole thing. I usually get a flood of negative emotions with a ghostly visit: injustice, anger, sadness. With Ethan? Just a typical teenager, happy-go-lucky even. Very rare for a newly dead ghost, and even rarer for a murder victim."

Miguel seemed to think about what Daphne was saying, but Ethan could only shrug. He felt what he felt.

"Perhaps it's all connected," Miguel stated. "He doesn't remember his death, so how could he be upset about it? Maybe he just feels what he felt when he was hanging out with his buddies. The last thing he remembers."

Daphne couldn't deny that Ethan's case was unique. She frowned as she mulled it over. Every death she encountered was unique in its own way, but Ethan was especially different. Nevertheless, she didn't feel she had the right to judge that any more than Miguel did. He could remember what he could remember and how could he be angry about something he was completely ignorant of? Daphne decided to embrace Ethan's approach to the whole thing and shrugged it off. For now.

"After you, detective," Daphne said, gesturing to the large front door. And Miguel continued with the reason they were there. He was on a clock, after all.

Miguel's knock was greeted by a handsome

middle-aged couple.  They were dressed like people who had nothing to do all day but go to the country club and Daphne resisted the urge to make a gagging face.  But more than that, they were both especially attractive. Daphne had a flash to her days growing up in Hollywood and knew these two would fit right in with that crowd.

"Detective Miguel Alvarez, Fresno P.D."  Miguel flashed his badge as he spoke, leaving no room for all the questions about why they were randomly at the door. "This is Daphne Winters, Police Consultant."  It wasn't technically true, yet, but in the works enough that he figured he could stretch a bit.

They barely reacted.  "How can we help you, detective?" the gentleman asked.

"We're actually hoping we could speak to a Tyra Cruz, if she's available."

"Oh."  The woman looked up at her husband. "She isn't here right now."

Suddenly the man, who'd been uninterested a moment ago, crossed his arms over his chest in a bit of a defensive stance.  His voice was still casual, but Daphne could sense this was just a standard level of concern rather than an evasion of some kind of justice.  These two knew their daughter could do no wrong.  "What's this about?" he asked.

Miguel looked at Daphne, debating whether or not to keep the details to himself, but Daphne nodded him on.  She knew these two weren't hiding anything.  "We believe she was potentially the last person to see a young man named Ethan Bender alive."

"Jake's friend?  Who committed suicide?"  The woman looked horrified at the thought of her daughter mixed up with such a scandal.

"Jake's friend," Miguel nodded as he confirmed, "who most likely did not take his own life, actually.  That's why we're hoping to talk to Tyra."  He opened a notebook from his front pocket and, even though he didn't need to consult his notes in any capacity, it did look very official.  "She was seen around eleven p.m. the night of Ethan's death picking him up from the Puente residence. We need to know what happened next."

"Our Tyra?" The confused parents exchanged a look, before Mrs. Cruz stated, "We weren't even aware she knew Ethan."

Miguel nodded. "Yes, Jake also told us they weren't close. So you can understand why we'd wonder why he called her to come pick him up. Shortly before he died."

He let the words dangle in the air, a puzzle with dark holes where pieces should go. The parents were shocked, concerned, but had nothing to say. So they stood there silently.

"So I need to speak to Tyra. Can you let us know where she is?" Miguel continued when they offered no assistance.

"Um, sure." That seemed to break them from their stupor. Mr. Cruz, arms still crossing his chest, told Miguel and Daphne, "She's at the Fresno State campus library. Working on her culminating project. She's going to law school." He said it so much on autopilot that it sounded robotic.

"Here.  Let me write her number down for you," Mrs. Cruz added.

When they were all back in the car—Daphne, Miguel and Ethan's ghost—Miguel turned to Daphne. "They really know nothing, do they?"

Daphne shook her head.  "They see the superstar they raised and nothing more.  Which might be all she is.  Again, I don't sense anything so far with this family that raises my suspicions."

"She's super smart," Ethan blurted out.  Daphne turned to where he appeared to her in the backseat, even though Miguel wasn't part of the conversation.  "Tyra.  She's smart and driven.  She wants to go into politics, be the first female president or something.  She's squeaky clean."

"I believe you.  But we're still curious why you called her. And then died."  Daphne frowned at Ethan.

"Maybe I just had a crush on her.  I always wanted to be the First Gentleman."  Ethan wiggled an eyebrow.

"You'd have been a good politician in your own right," Daphne said.  She was simply stating what she sensed, but he took it as a compliment.

"Thanks."  Ethan flashed a handsome everybody-likes-me smile.  "But I can tell you one thing for sure. Tyra did *not* kill me.  No way."

Daphne agreed.  "I don't get that sense either. But could she know who did?"

Ethan didn't respond.

"I only have ten minutes," Miguel announced, interrupting the conversation he couldn't join anyway. "Can you take me back to HQ?  I can call Tyra from the station."

Daphne shook her head.  "Nope.  This one I need to do face-to-face.  I need to sense the things she *doesn't* tell us."

"Then I'll send Gina back out with you."

Daphne shook her head.  "I can do this alone.  If I uncover anything juicy, I promise I'll hand it off neatly to you and Gina."

Miguel laughed as he said, "You're a handful, Daphne Winters."

Daphne smiled when she said, "But you love me anyway."

Miguel was still smiling as he said, "The official report is suicide anyway.  So technically, you're not working an official case."  He wagged a finger at her.  "But promise me one thing.  Do not go running off into criminal rings on your own.  You call me if you uncover anything sinister. Understood?"

Daphne stared at him like he was being unreasonable, but she didn't exactly promise she wouldn't put her life in danger.  They both knew she would if she felt she needed to.  "Let me at least find out what kind of trouble this kid got himself into."

Daphne missed Miguel the minute she dropped him off downtown.  She was used to doing things on her own and had done for years.  But now that she had Miguel, she found that she really enjoyed him coming with her. Yes, he gave her questioning of witnesses a validity she didn't have on her own. But it was more than that.

He grounded her.

But he was stuck on desk duty while he healed from his gunshot wound and she was rogue. Even if she was acting in an official capacity, she'd be rogue. And also she was really darn curious. What had happened to Ethan Bender? This even-keeled, calm- as-a-summer-breeze ghost who couldn't remember his own death.

The Fresno State campus was much bigger than Daphne expected. Not that Daphne had a ton of experience on college campuses, but for some reason she expected to find a small local agricultural school. Fresno was nestled in the heart of California's Central Valley where much of the state's food was grown. Surrounding the town were miles and miles of orchards and grapevines and corn husks as far as the eye could see.

But Fresno State turned out to be more like a small town. And the library looked more like a high-rise office building than a cozy library.  After walking in and looking up at the high ceilings, Daphne decided she would need her senses if she was going to find Tyra anytime soon.

"She's pre-law, so I say we go this way."  Ethan was already heading toward a staircase.  Daphne saw no reason to argue and followed the ghost.  When he got to a section on "Civic Government," he started looking around for the familiar face.  "There!" he shouted, although only Daphne could hear him, and pointed at a corner table where a young girl was sitting with a book open, a notebook out and headphones on.

Daphne nodded to Ethan in thanks and walked over to Tyra's table.  She plopped down in the chair across from the young girl with the mocha skin and smiled.  She wanted to be friendly, but it looked more like a crocodile's grin.

Ethan leaned in to Daphne.  "Don't scare her off."

"I'm Daphne," Daphne announced to Tyra.  The young girl removed her headphones, saying nothing, but a look of complete curiosity and bewilderment took over her face.  Daphne instantly realized why Ethan might want to hang around this smart girl.  She was stunning.  Beauty and brains?  These two might have been a power couple if they had been given the chance.  "Do you believe in ghosts?"

Tyra wrinkled her brow in confusion, still saying nothing.  She wanted to be angry about the interruption, but her curiosity was at war with her frustration.

"I'm a psychic medium and I've been in contact with Ethan Bender.  Remember him?" Daphne asked.

"Of course I do."  Tyra's voice was barely more than a whisper.  She was hooked now.  No way was she leaving until she knew where all this was headed.

"The night of his death, he hung out with your cousin Jake.  Then he went to a drug dealer's party.  And then he called you.  Somehow, he ended up dead, but he doesn't remember the details.  Although he is fairly certain he did not take his own life.  So I'm curious if you have details you could help fill in."

Tyra took in a deep breath before saying, "He didn't call me."

Daphne leaned in.  She could tell Tyra was telling the truth.  "He didn't?  You gave him a ride, right?"

Tyra nodded.  "But I called him."

"I knew it.  She couldn't resist me."  Ethan's ghost was beaming where he stood next to the two ladies. Daphne looked up at him and rolled her eyes.

"Did you know he was with drug dealers?  Were you trying to help him?" Daphne asked.

Tyra shook her head.  "How on earth could I know he was with drug dealers?  No.  I called him because I needed *him*."

"But you barely knew him, right?  That's what Jake said.  What did you need him for?"

Tyra stared at Daphne for a moment, and Daphne could sense she was trying to decide how much to tell her.  She didn't owe Daphne anything.  Daphne was just a random person, especially without Miguel or Gina here to make the questioning official.

After a moment, Tyra asked, "Daphne, is it?" When Daphne nodded, Tyra continued.  "Daphne, my reasons for needing Ethan that night are between him and me.  I can assure you it had nothing to do with Ethan's death, so unless you are a psychic police detective with a badge and a warrant, I have nothing else to say to you."

Tyra continued looking at her book, placing her headphones back in her ears and thereby essentially dismissing Daphne.

And then Ethan snapped his fingers.  "That's right!  She called me!  She needed my help breaking into the pawn shop."

"Breaking into a pawn shop?"  Daphne was actually shocked, so her voice was unnecessarily loud and echoed throughout the expansive library.

But it definitely got Tyra's attention.  She pulled her headphones out of her ears and leaned in to Daphne. "What did you say?"

"Ethan just told me you enlisted his services for a

little late night breaking and entering.  Care to elaborate on this one?"

Tyra closed her book, assuming the studying she was trying to accomplish wasn't happening at the moment.  She slipped her notebook in her backpack, stuck her phone and headphones in her pocket and stood up.  "Come with me."

"So now you believe me?"  Daphne shook her head as she stood and followed Tyra out of the library.

Tyra spoke over her shoulder as she spoke.  "It's not that I didn't believe you, necessarily.  I just didn't think it was any of your business.  Big difference."

Daphne knew she was telling the truth, and she was right, so she said nothing in response.  Daphne found herself appreciating this intelligent beauty.  She was no-nonsense and tough as nails.  Daphne's kind of person.

As they walked, Ethan began to voice the things he was remembering.  "She needed something from the pawn shop.  Westside Trade and Loan.  That was the place.  She knew I had a certain set of skills and I wasn't related to her, so that made me the perfect person to call."

"What skills?"  Daphne asked Ethan, but Tyra thought she meant her, so she responded.

"Ethan's skills?"  Tyra asked when they were outside.  She continued walking toward the parking lot.

Daphne decided to answer Tyra.  "Yes.  Why did you call Ethan?  I still don't understand."

Tyra sighed.  "This is my car.  Let's talk in here."  She unlocked it and Tyra and Daphne climbed inside.  "I really don't want my school knowing the details of my side project."

"Side project?" Daphne asked.  So far, she knew Tyra was being truthful, but breaking into a store didn't really fit the image of the beautiful, smart and determined young lady with a bright future.

"I've been working with the non-profit Angels of Freedom.  Ever heard of them?"

Daphne shook her head just as the image of convicted felons popped into her mind.

Tyra continued. "We help people who have been wrongfully convicted overturn their convictions and get justice."

"Okay. That sounds noble enough. Why were you breaking the law to help people who supposedly didn't break the law?" Daphne asked. "And why Ethan?"

"I've been helping a man named Octavio Torres. He went to prison for a murder he didn't commit. Luckily, he just got life instead of the death penalty, so we have time to gather the evidence to get him freed."

"How do you know he is innocent?"

"He has an alibi. He's always had one. The police and prosecutors just never followed up on it. They had their man, case closed."

Daphne looked skeptical. "That doesn't seem right. Why wouldn't they check his alibi? That's shoddy police work." She sensed her own defensiveness rise up as an image of Miguel popped into her mind. Impeccable, strait-laced Miguel. He would never ignore someone's alibi.

"Daphne. Justice works differently for people like you than for some people. It's not shoddy police work. It's easy. Or they're protecting someone. I'm not exactly sure which just yet."

"Okay. So, this Octavio Torres is an innocent man behind bars. What's in the pawn shop?"

Tyra sighed. "Not that it's any of your business, but I also know you can't legally hold any of this against me."

Daphne snorted. "And also I don't care. I'm just here for Ethan."

Tyra shrugged. "And also you don't care." She seemed to debate something for a second before asking, "Who exactly are you again?"

"I'm a psychic medium working with the Fresno Police Department homicide division. I've been in contact with Ethan Bender's ghost and none of us accept that he committed suicide."

Tyra nodded. If she doubted anything Daphne said, she had a great poker face. "Got it. Suicide never made sense, so I'm glad the truth will be investigated." Tyra turned back toward Daphne, shifting in the driver's seat to face her full on. "There's a street thug named Sharky. Pretty well known in the Fresno street scene. He's the real murderer of Thang Nguyen, not Octavio Torres. But Sharky has been hard to catch. Or he's an informant. Anyway, he used a gun to kill Thang, but there was a knife also used in that attack. Police have the gun, but the knife was in the Westside Trade and Loan. Enough people know that knife as Sharky's, plus I am *sure* there is some DNA evidence, that I thought it would be enough to get him a re-trial."

A flash of a long knife with a jade handle flew into Daphne's mind. It was beautiful, but Daphne wouldn't want it held up to her throat. "So why Ethan?"

Tyra made a face like the reason should be obvious. "Jake and Ethan loved to go snooping around old, abandoned buildings and all. Many of them fenced off or completely shuttered. They called it urban exploring. If they could do that and never get caught, I knew Ethan could get in and get me my knife undetected."

"But wouldn't your non-profit be willing to just buy it?  Why risk getting caught?"  Daphne folded her arms.

Tyra shook her head.  "They can't procure evidence.  It would be thrown out."

"So did it work?"

Tyra looked crestfallen.  "No.  We never broke in. We sat outside the pawn shop for an hour, debating the philosophical right and wrong of doing bad things for good reasons.  In the end, it just didn't seem right."

Daphne frowned.  So he goes to all these random places in the middle of the night, but none of them have anything to do with his death?  "So, then you took him home?"

Tyra shook her head.  "No.  He said he had something to do and that I should go home.  He got out of my car right there.  I had a really bad feeling, but he just kept telling me to go home.  I know it sounds awful now that he's gone, but I didn't know what else to do.  I drove home."

Daphne couldn't put her finger on it, but something felt sinister.  "That's where you died, isn't it?  You walked toward the danger?"  She had turned to Ethan in the backseat and Tyra followed her gaze.  Tyra saw nothing.

When Ethan shrugged, Daphne turned back to Tyra.

"Tyra, can you please tell me how to get to the Westside Trade and Loan?  I have this nagging sense that Ethan died there."

# 10.

"Oh, Miguel." Gina's face was ashen white. She was clearly distressed over something and that instantly put Miguel on alert. His partner was the more laid back of the two, so if she was worried, he was worried. "It's really bad."

"Oh, my God, Gina. What?" Miguel couldn't even bring himself to sit at his desk. He was too nervous. Instead, he just paced around Gina like a mad man.

"As punishment for the altercation between Sheffley and Tigre this morning, I am partnered with Sheffley for the foreseeable future."

"What?"  Miguel had been expecting something about Ethan Bender, or Victor Cruz and the drive-by. Maybe another homicide or someone they had once helped put away was out now and hunting them.  This? His partner being reassigned?  Nowhere in his capacity for reason.

Gina nodded.  "Apparently, my sin was in not training him well.  Which, I will admit, is true.  I mostly ignored him.  But this?  This is way more awful of a punishment than I was expecting."

"So what do I do in the meantime?  Shuffle paperwork?"  Miguel was almost yelling.  Almost.  His face was definitely hot.

Gina rolled her eyes.  "Yes.  You aren't cleared for fieldwork anyway."  Gina pulled Miguel down to his seat, and then she leaned in.  "Look, I am really not happy about this either.  He basically turned it around on me and made me look like *I* screwed up somehow.  He should be on leave for his racist conduct.  But I have to make this right.  For the sake of my own career."  She leaned back.

"And I have an idea."

Miguel regarded Gina for a moment, not sure he even wanted to hear her idea.  He just wanted to be back at his job one hundred percent and out there with Gina doing what they did best.  Now, he felt as if he'd been left behind somehow.  He spoke with no enthusiasm.  "I'm listening."

"You keep doing what you're doing with the Ethan Bender case.  Support Daphne and do as much as you can from your desk."  Gina leaned back.  "Meanwhile, I'll keep working the Victor Cruz drive-by with Greenie and hopefully when we're done, The Sarge will think he's so amazing he can have a new partner.  Then you and I get back to the rest of this pile."

Miguel shook his head.  "I don't think it's going to be that easy.  You oversimplify things sometimes."

Gina cocked her head to the side.  "And you overthink things and are generally a pain in my ass, but I still enjoy working with you.  Do you have a better idea, tough guy?"

Miguel swiveled his chair away from Gina. "Nope. It was good while it lasted."

Gina grabbed the closest thing she could find, which turned out to be a paper clip, and threw it at Miguel's head. He didn't even flinch. What was he going to do pushing papers from his desk? He silently cursed Judge Bustamante in his head. If it hadn't been for that fat arrogant bastard and his crime syndicate, things would still be as they were.

"Howdy partner!" Sheffley sauntered up to Gina's desk with a large grin. She tightened her lips in an effort to avoid calling him a name or physically assaulting him. She was mad at him, but she was mad at herself also for not just taking the time that morning. This could all be over with if she had just sucked it up and trained the newbie.

"Here." Gina handed Sheffley the papers she'd been given that morning from Spencer. "Call these people. They own the purple El Camino with the flames. The one identified at the drive-by this morning."

"Call? Isn't there a uniformed officer for junk work?" Sheffley scoffed.

"You want to find the bad guy? You gotta roll up your sleeves. This is the job." Gina put her hands on her hips and forced herself to speak as calmly and professionally as she could. "We need to know if they are related to Sharky in any way, if the car was stolen, if they're accomplices, yada yada."

"And what are you going to do?" Sheffley stuck his chin out, his smug attitude still making it evident that he thought this request was beneath him. Miguel could only inwardly groan. He was a seasoned detective and that was all he'd be doing until his shoulder healed.

"I'm going to dig into Tigre, Gordito and Mula. See if I can find out why Victor Cruz was the target and they got off scot-free." Gina narrowed her eyes. Something about all of this seemed fishy.

"Why can't we do both? Together as a team?" Sheffley asked.

Gina rolled her eyes. "You can't be anywhere

near Tigre again.  Anyway, if you can track down Sharky, we've got our man.  That's a very important job."  First of all, she meant it.  Secondly, a little male ego stroking never hurt anyone.

And it worked.  Sheffley puffed out his chest and said, "Why didn't you just start with 'find Sharky'?  I'm on it."

"Perfect," Gina smiled, satisfied to finally be getting somewhere with this guy.

When Sheffley was out of earshot, Miguel spoke just above a whisper to Gina.  "Is that guy for real?"

Gina shook her head.  "Probably saw one too many of Daphne's dad's movies."

Miguel laughed at that, since Beck Winters *had* made his share of police adventure movies, over-dramatizing everything with car chases as the primary means of catching the bad guy.

"Speaking of which, what is Daphne up to?" Gina asked.

"She's getting the scoop from Tyra right now,"

Miguel explained.

"On her own?"

Miguel nodded.  "I ran out of time on my lunch hour."  He used air quotes to denote the clever ruse of his lunch hour.  "But she's approaching it as a psychic, not as a detective.  As of right now, we still have no reason to say anything other than suicide."

Gina regarded her former partner.  "Okay."  She grabbed her car keys from her desk.  "I guess at the end of the day, I've got my hands full with Sheffley and Sharky anyway."

"I would agree there."  Miguel leaned back in his chair.  "Do you want me to make any calls for you?  I can at least do that much.  And then you can have some more quality time with your protégé."

Gina flipped Miguel off, but then answered in earnest. "Yeah, maybe.  I may have you double-check the greenie's work.  The purple El Camino was registered to a couple in their fifties who take their car to car shows and such.  I don't see them being complicit in a drive-by, but they must be connected to Sharky somehow."

"Are we sure Sharky is the culprit?" Miguel asked. "You said yourself you thought Tigre was sketchy."

Gina pointed a finger at Miguel. "This is why I love you. You're right. Once you're a liar, you're a liar. His whole story could be misdirection. I need to talk to him." Gina seemed to debate something internally before asking, "Do you think I could have Daphne assist? To make sure he's telling the truth?"

Miguel smiled. He was beyond proud of Daphne and her talents. And he also thought it was a brilliant idea. "I think she'd be happy to help."

"I never really got a statement from anyone, since Sheffley mucked it all up. But what he'd told me was Sharky drove by in a purple El Camino with flames on it and shot *only* Victor Cruz. The one other guy who was barely scratched was supposedly just collateral damage."

"So, no matter what, Victor Cruz was the target?" Miguel asked.

"So they tell me," Gina responded.

"Then let me research what I can about Victor Cruz. See if I can find a reason someone would want him dead. I'll work on that while you talk to Tigre with Daphne and find out if he's lying."

"Glad you could make yourself useful," Gina stated with a sarcastic smile.

"I can't take a bullet for you every day," Miguel responded, but he was smiling as he did.

"I'll have Daphne meet me at the jail. We'll call with an update in a bit. If you get anything, anything at all, call me." Gina started heading out.

"Good luck," Miguel muttered as he started searching for Victor Cruz in his database. He was fairly certain that with Daphne on her side, Gina wouldn't need any luck at all. Good chance they'd have Victor himself to let them know what happened that fateful morning.

# 11.

"I was on my way to the Westside Trade and Loan to see where Ethan died," Daphne explained to Gina over the phone.

"Please," Gina pleaded. "We can go together to the pawn shop right after. I don't think this will take too long. I just need your intuition on this guy's story. Something doesn't sit right with me."

Daphne almost said no; she really wanted to. Although she knew there was another murder victim she could help find justice, she was really focused on Ethan's case. He had no idea how he'd died, which was unusual.

And he was seemingly at peace with his young death, which was very unusual. All of this intrigued Daphne as much as solving the mystery of his death.

"You should go. Help her," Ethan said to Daphne. He stood next to her with his arms folded. He was so calm and confident. Just no care in the world about taking a backseat to another case when his own was still so ambiguous.

Daphne gave him a side eye, but then relinquished. If he could take a step back, then so could she. After all, he had eternity to get answers.

Daphne sighed. "Okay. Meet ya at the jail."

As Gina waited for Daphne, she decided to get started with Tigre. This time he was in a cell alone without his compadres. At least this would allow her to focus.

"Remember me, Tigre? Or can I call you Anthony?" Gina asked. She had seen his rap sheet. Anthony "Tigre" Villalobos had been in and out of the system since he was twelve. A real model citizen. And he was young, so there was lots more mischief for him to get into before he was too old.

Or died living as he did.

Tigre shrugged.  He didn't want this lady cop to know that he didn't think "Anthony" sounded tough.  He didn't want her to know that he'd adopted the street name after he'd been in a small scuffle with a neighborhood boy who'd been talking trash.  In the fight, Anthony had scratched the kid's face, deep and scarring. The bystanders had called him a tiger for the maneuver, and he'd stuck with it ever since.

"Let's forget what happened this morning, okay? I still want to get to the bottom of what happened to Victor.  Can you start at the beginning and tell me what happened?" Gina asked.

"It was early, but we'd been up all night hanging out and stuff.  But then we got the munchies and decided to go to the mini mart on the corner by my house.  That's when Sharky pulled up and shot at us."

"So everyone had been hanging out at your

house?"

Tigre nodded. "Yes."

"And can you give me the names of 'everyone'? Who all had been hanging out?"

"Me. Victor. Gordito and Mula."

"And what exactly had you been doing?  Before the early morning stroll?"

Tigre shrugged.  "Hanging out.  Smoking pot and shit.  Nothing big."

Gina frowned.  So far she believed him.  "Okay. When you were shot at, how did you know it was Sharky?"

Tigre tossed his head back as if she were asking the world's dumbest question.  "I saw him!  He didn't even try to hide it.  He leaned out the window as he shot the gun."

"So Sharky was driving?"

"Yeah, man.  He slowed down just long enough to shoot at us and then took off."

"Was anyone else in the car?  The purple El

Camino?"

Tigre shook his head dramatically.  "No.  Just Sharky."

Gina was just about to announce how little she believed this part of the story when Daphne walked into the holding area.  Ethan followed closely behind, but no one else could see him.

"This is Daphne Winters."  Gina gestured to the spiky-haired blonde.  "She's a psychic who sometimes helps on these types of cases."

"A what?"  Tigre looked like he'd smelled something foul, scrunching his nose and wrinkling his face.

"It means I am in tune with the spiritual world and our sixth sense. So if you're lying, I'll know."  Daphne smiled.  Without much other context she could instantly sense this guy was trouble.  And that there were holes in whatever story he was trying to spin.

"That's bullshit."  Tigre waved a hand at Daphne, but it just made her smile more.  This guy wasn't even a challenge.

Gina was just about to start digging into the actual events of the drive-by when her phone rang. Seeing it was her new partner, Sheffley, she decided it was best if she ignored her instincts and answered. "Detective Malone."

"Gina.  This definitely wasn't the car.  The Alecantes weren't even in Fresno at the time.  They and their purple El Camino were at a car show in Palm Springs.  I have surveillance video being sent to me now showing their car was there."

"Good work, Sheffley."  And she meant it.  "So you know what this means?"

Sheffley huffed.  "Yeah.  That witness is full of shit."

Gina nodded.  "My thoughts exactly.  I'm getting Tigre's full statement now, so I'll share notes with you when I am back."  And then she added for good measure, "Partner."

When Gina hung up, she stared at Tigre for a

moment.  "If I interview Mula and Gordito, will their story match up exactly to yours?"

Tigre's smug face made Gina want to smack him.  "They won't talk to no cops."

"We'll see about that."  Gina put her hands on her hips.  "Care to explain how you saw the purple El Camino driven by Sharky when the purple El Camino you described was in Palm Springs that morning?"

Tigre shrugged, unfazed.  "There must be two."

"It's not a white Honda Civic.  Purple El Caminos stand out in the registration database," Gina explained.

"Victor owed you money," Daphne blurted out at Tigre, and his eyes snapped to hers.  His eyes widened for just a moment before he recovered and put back on the show of not being intimidated by lady cops.

This guy had spent years perfecting the art of pretending nothing bothered him.

"And?  So?  Lots of people owe me money." Tigre stuck out his chin, but Daphne could see the cracks in the façade that no one else could see.

Tigre was scared.  They were getting too close.

Flashes of yelling, glasses breaking, and fists swinging raced through Daphne's mind.  "You got into a fight with Victor at your apartment.  He didn't back down and so you shot him."  Daphne waved a finger at Tigre.  "Never could manage that temper, could you?"

"Are you saying that if we compare the bullet he shot at Sheffley this morning to the ones that killed Victor Cruz they will match?"  Gina asked Daphne, her eyes locked on the man in the jail cell she had been suspicious of the whole day.

Daphne reached for the answer.

When she was in Hollywood, she had perfected the skill of reaching inside someone's mind.  She was loathe to do it, but it did have some advantages.  She pushed into Tigre's thoughts and dug through his memories until she found the events of that night.

"He shot Victor at his apartment.  He and his friends carried him to the street and invented the drive-by story.  Then they tossed the murder weapon into a dumpster near the mini mart on the corner."  Daphne's eyes were closed as she recounted the events.

"Wham, bam, thank you ma'am."  Gina smiled. Daphne had just given her a play-by-play of the actual events.  "Looks like we already have our culprit right here behind bars.  We'll just add first-degree murder to your assaulting a police officer charge and get you locked up for good."

Tigre scoffed.  "Some dumb lady's story is going to put me away?  I don't think so."

"Maybe, maybe not.  But I suspect the murder weapon in the dumpster and the forensics in your apartment will," Gina responded.  She texted Sheffley to get started on the warrant.

"It was a lot of money," Ethan told Daphne.

Daphne looked over her shoulder at Ethan.  How did he know this Tigre case when he barely knew his own?  "What?"

Gina looked at the blank space behind Daphne, assuming correctly that she was talking to a spirit.

"Ethan?" Daphne nodded in response.

"This is the guy." Ethan smiled as he said it. Like he always did, he just had this charismatic nonchalance like nothing could ever get to him. "That case against Octavio Torres that Tyra is working? This is the guy who paid Sharky to kill Thang."

Daphne shook her head. She tried to use her psychic intuition to read Ethan, but it was a brick wall.

She was so confused. "Do you mind explaining how on earth you could know all this?"

"They were both there that night at the Westside Trade and Loan." Ethan stuck his chin out to indicate the murderer behind bars. "Tigre and Sharky. He just tried to throw Sharky under the bus for his own indiscretion, but they're partners. Victor owed them close to ten grand. I heard it all the night I died."

Daphne couldn't hide her shock. "What? What exactly are you telling me?"

Ethan pushed off the wall. "It's time you know the full truth. This is the man who killed me and dumped me off the overpass.  Tigre murdered me that night at the pawn shop."

# 12.

"Murdered you?  Now you suddenly remember everything?" Daphne asked, her shock overwhelming her. Being blindsided by information was a very rare event. She was not handling it well.

"What?  What's happening?"  Gina could only stare at Daphne's reaction.  She had no idea what Ethan was saying.

"I always did remember everything," Ethan said with a shrug.  "But my parents deserve the truth and if I simply *told* you the details, they wouldn't have believed you.  I needed you to discover it with corroboration."

His laid-back tone and vibe were refreshing in a

lot of ways, but right now it was pushing Daphne to the edge of where she could keep a lid on her frustration. She had to form fists to keep from shaking.

"He says Tigre and Sharky murdered him.  Ethan just said that," Daphne explained to Gina.

"No way."  Gina matched Daphne in her shocked expression. Tigre was just a witness a few hours ago, and now he was the prime suspect in two cases they were working?  It just seemed so unlikely as to border on the ridiculous.  Gina turned to Tigre in his cell.  "Did you kill a teenaged boy a couple weeks ago?"

Tigre just stared at her like she was talking crazy, but he neither confirmed nor denied.

"Start talking, Bender."  Daphne put her hands on her hips, her long skirt swaying with her movement.  She liked Ethan, genuinely did.  But right now, she was highly annoyed with him.

"I was going to fill you in when we got to the pawn shop.  Honest."  Ethan smiled, and right now if it wasn't so infuriating to Daphne, it would be endearing.

"But he ran me over with his car.  Sharky was in the passenger seat."

Daphne shook her head.  She couldn't sense any of this, and that drove her crazy.  She knew her skills had gotten even better since honing them so much when she was looking for Maddy in Southern California.  But it was more than that.  How did he go from helping Tyra to being run over by a car?  "This makes no sense, Ethan.  How do you know that this is the guy?  And how am I not able to sense what you know?  Ghosts can never hide things from me, even when they want to.  It just...comes out of them whether they like it or not."

"Welllll...."  Ethan dragged the word out as he leaned against the wall.  He was still so casual and laid back.  Daphne didn't know whether to love that about him or hate it.  "About that.  I also was going to tell you that...well, I'm not a ghost.  Not a typical one anyway."

Daphne had to hold her hands up in the air in an effort to get the room to stop spinning from the weird bits of information that were spewing from Ethan's mouth. She could feel her frustration rising and that usually meant she was about to start yelling. "I'm sorry, but I call it bullshit. You were a teenager who died. Ergo, a ghost."

"What? What is happening?" Gina couldn't help but watch and feel a strong desire to hear both sides. And seeing Daphne about to lose it with a ghost was a very uncommon event, so it intrigued her all the more.

"He's telling me he's not a ghost." Daphne rolled her eyes as she explained to Gina.

"Y'all are nuts," Tigre added from behind them, but everyone ignored him.

Suddenly, Gina was uncomfortable having this conversation in front of her murder suspect. She didn't want any public defenders getting him off on some technicalities about star witnesses being crazy or something. "Let's have this conversation in the hallway." She ushered Daphne into the hallway, and Ethan followed.

The door had barely closed behind them when

Daphne turned to Ethan, her hands on her hips.

"I'm an angel," Ethan blurted in response. "Every so often, God lets us have a turn as a human." He shrugged. "I got the chance to be Ethan Bender."

Daphne waved her hands again. "Hold on. You're telling me that your soul isn't human? But you paraded around as a human for seventeen years?"

Ethan nodded. "That's the truth."

"No. Just, no." Daphne shook her head in disbelief. "I've been talking to spirits all my life. I've never encountered a dead angel."

"I'm sorry. A what?" Gina struggled to keep up and her mind was spinning.

"You've experienced angels before," Ethan told her. "We can feel very much like human spirits. But we're more powerful. And in our angel form, not as susceptible to human emotions." He smiled again, so casual, and this time it softened Daphne. She had to admit, she had known he was different from the start. She just didn't know he was *this* different.

"Okay, smartass.  Let's say I believe that you're an angel who got a chance to be human," Daphne started.

Ethan responded, "And that's the truth."

"How did your angelic ass end up dead at seventeen?  Don't you have special powers to live longer than most?"

Ethan shook his head.  "Not in human form.  And anyway, that wasn't the deal."

Daphne couldn't hide her frustration.  She squeaked out an exasperated grunt as she asked, "What deal?"

"My deal with God.  I told you.  Sometimes he lets us have a chance to be human.  We get to be born, have a family, face hunger and feel stress.  Have love, play baseball.  I *really loved* playing baseball.  It's a great opportunity. But it comes at a price. We have to promise to help others, even if it means sacrificing our own human lives.  When I got out of Tyra's car that night, I knew it was the end for me."

Daphne gushed out a huge sigh and turned to Gina. "So here's the story so far. He says he is really an angel who got the chance to be human, but in order to be human he had to make a deal with God that he would sacrifice his life if it came down to it."

Gina thought about Daphne's update for a moment, chewing on her lip. "Okay. I think that's believable."

"Is it?" Daphne wrinkled her eyebrow.

"Really? You of all people are being skeptical?" Gina laughed and it made Daphne frown. "It's not what we expected, for sure, but is it really *that* big of a leap from what you're used to?"

Daphne pouted. She actually pouted. "I guess not."

"It's more common than you know, Daphne. We're very good at playing our cards close to our chest," Ethan explained. "Angels are everywhere, but we can be interchangeable with human spirits if you don't know what you're looking for."

"Which is?" Daphne asked.  She was feeling a little lost and she hated not being in control.  Having surprise information thrown at her was very unusual, and it didn't sit right with her.  She wanted to learn so next time she could be in the know.

"Well, for starters we're much better at controlling our human emotions."  Ethan smiled as he again explained the reason Daphne hadn't been feeling anything from him as she usually did with most ghosts. Daphne had to admit that that much she had noticed was unique about him.  She'd noticed it from the start. Murder victims could have all kinds of feelings, and they usually were radiating from every pore when they came to Daphne. Ethan had been self-assured from the get-go. And that *had* been a red flag.  "And there's our aura. Look at me closely.  This time, I bet you see it."

Daphne took a step back and stared at Ethan Bender.  She rarely felt the need to read someone's aura, but they did occasionally give her insight into their soul. And now that she looked carefully at Ethan's, she could see it.  Humans were multi-colored, glowing in various shades of the rainbow, different colors meaning different vibes that spoke about the human specifically.  And the color combinations could be as varied and complex as humans themselves.

Ethan's was golden.  Solid gold.  Ethan Bender was an angel.

When he saw the recognition in Daphne's eyes, Ethan continued.  "I'm a guardian angel.  Some of us are warriors, out fighting evil, preventing bad things from happening."  Ethan shook his head.  "There honestly aren't enough of those.  And there are transition angels.  They're the ones who help human souls into and out of life.  When you see a spirit hovering at someone's deathbed?  That's a transition angel.  Some angels are confined to Heaven, maintaining that system.  And it's a doozy, let me tell you.  But most of us walk among humans daily as guardian angels. That's me."

"I honestly had no idea.  Did you know you were an angel throughout your human life?" Daphne asked the smiling angel before her.  Now that she saw his golden hue, she couldn't unsee it.

"Not really."  Ethan shrugged.  "There were moments when I sensed I was different, but through the human emotions I just believed I was some extraordinary human. But that night. The night with Tyra. I don't know how to explain it.  It was like a calling.  I just *knew* suddenly what I had to do.  And I knew it wasn't going to end well for the human being, Ethan Bender."

"Okay. So fill me in on what happened that night. And how Tigre here ran you over with a car."  Daphne gestured back toward the room with the holding cell as she spoke.

"Okay."  Ethan pushed off the wall and his body language changed.  He was a storyteller now, and he was relieved to finally tell Daphne everything.  Holding it in earlier had been challenging at times.  "As you know, I was sitting in the car with Tyra, discussing ways to help her with her false conviction—which, by the way, is also true.  I didn't think she should break the law to help someone who didn't break the law.  But she can be very passionate."

"I did notice that about her," Daphne nodded.

"And it was like I said, I just *knew* what I was supposed to do.  It's hard to explain.  Almost like I was given instructions that I couldn't hear or see but that were implanted deep into my brain."

"I get that, too."  Daphne nodded along.  There were moments when even non-psychics could just be in tune with the world around them.  Like when you know the bad news before someone gives it.  Or when you just know the decision you are supposed to make even when you don't have much information.  You just *know*.

"I was drawn to the Westside Trade and Loan but not to break in.  I was drawn there because those two were attacking a young woman."  Ethan insinuated Tigre and Sharky.

"He says Tigre and Sharky were attacking a young woman," Daphne explained to Gina.  "The night he died."

Gina's eyes widened at the new revelation, but

she said nothing, assuming full well that Daphne would continue getting the scoop from the newly dead angel.

"Behind the pawn shop there is a narrow alley. I'd never been there before, but that night I saw it like an image in my mind.  I was told to go there," Ethan continued.  "Her name is Daniella.  I think Sharky must like knives because he had one at her throat and Tigre was trying to tie up her hands and feet.  They weren't going to let her live.  She would have died that night if I hadn't walked into that alley.  I know that's the truth."

"I believe you," Daphne nodded.  As he spoke, she got flashes of the scene in the alley.  She knew their plans for Daniella were not wholesome.  Ethan saved her from the worst night of her life getting even worse.

"I had no idea what I was going to do when I got there, but after I told Tyra to leave, I ran straight to the alley behind the Westside Trade and Loan.  And I saw what I knew I'd see."  Ethan sighed.  "Daniella was so scared.  I can still feel her fear.  But the second I turned the corner into the alley, the two men moved their focus to me.  And Tigre hadn't finished tying her up, so she was able to escape with barely a knick under her chin from Sharky's knife."  Ethan looked right into Daphne's eyes.  "I don't say this for glory, I only say it so you know.  It was my fate to trade my life for hers that night."

"Ethan interrupted the attack and the girl went free," Daphne explained to Gina.  "And then Sharky and Tigre turned their attention to Ethan."

"Once I knew she was free, I turned and ran.  And of course, the guys chased me.  Now it was sport as much as destroying a witness.  They hopped into a black Honda Civic—not a purple El Camino—and ran me down.  It was up on the sidewalk, so the tire marks are still there.  In fact, if you order an autopsy, there will probably be tire marks on my back.  They backed up, ran over me again.  And then to cover their tracks, tossed me off the overpass. The mangling from being hit by the car plus the mangling from falling from so great a height, made it difficult to immediately think murder."

"They drove a black Honda Civic the night they

killed Ethan," Daphne told Gina. "And there might even be tire marks near the pawn shop."

"So if we find the car, we might get physical evidence from hitting Ethan?" Gina asked.

"Yeah, possibly. I guess we need to find Sharky. And Daniella, the victim they originally intended to hurt that night. And I'd really like to head to the pawn shop."

Gina nodded. "This guy's not going anywhere." She gestured toward where they had left Tigre in the holding cell. "Do we have a last name for Daniella?"

Daphne looked at Ethan, but the name popped in her head as she did, and she spoke at the same time as Ethan. "Santos."

Gina turned to call her newbie partner, Sheffley, and Ethan continued talking to Daphne. "She is going to open an animal shelter. Daniella. In twelve years. Her passion for animals will drive her to open a safe place for people to take unwanted pets or strays found on the streets."

"She sounds like a good person," Daphne told

Ethan.  She wasn't much of an animal lover herself, but she certainly respected that they should be cared for and loved.

"Exactly," Ethan beamed.  "She has a purpose that she needs to live for.  This world needs her."

"True, but don't sell yourself short, Ethan.  People here are devastated by your death.  Your life had purpose, too."  Daphne frowned.  Even though she knew he'd be fine in the hereafter, the loss of a young life never made her happy.

But Ethan continued smiling proudly.  "I did have a purpose.  I gave up my life for Daniella's that night in the alley.  And *that* was my purpose."  He leaned in to whisper to Daphne for some unknown reason.  As if anyone else could even hear him.  "So, in a way, her animal shelter is mine, too."

Daphne just shook her head.  This kid.  No, this *angel*.  What a bizarre day this was turning out to be.

"All right, let's head to the pawn shop."  Gina nodded toward the exit.  "I've got Spencer chasing down the car-slash-murder-weapon and Sheffley looking for Sharky. Miguel is calling Daniella.  I can't believe these two teenagers are responsible for so many deaths."

"Don't judge them too harshly.  Even misguided people do what they think is best," Ethan answered Gina, though only to Daphne.

"Shut up, Ethan," Daphne responded.

"Shutting up."

# 13.

"This is the guy."  Sheffley handed a printout of a mug shot to Spencer.  "Shawn 'Sharky' Zaman.  For only being twenty years old, he's got a rap sheet a mile long.  Grand theft auto, larceny, assault, resisting arrest.  Real model citizen."

"Hmmm….    Yeah, there's no car formally registered to this guy.  Although can't say that I'm surprised.  I doubt he registers the vehicles after he steals them.  I can pull the list of black Honda Civics reported missing in the past six months in the greater Fresno area, but that list will likely be long."

"What are the odds he's still driving it?"  Sheffley spoke his thoughts out loud.

"Probably not great.  A career criminal like this one probably tosses cars fairly regularly to avoid capture. Especially one he used to kill someone."  Spencer began typing, searching for all the possible cars for Sheffley to begin hunting down.

"Pull me this guy's address, anyway.  He's a person of interest, so I need him brought in for questioning.  Maybe we'll get lucky and he'll talk." Sheffley sighed.  He didn't really think he was going to get lucky.

"Ya know, there's a forensics team at Tigre's apartment.  That drive-by you and Detective Malone were called out to?  Not a drive-by.  I guess the murder took place inside."

"I know," Sheffley responded.  "I'm the one who sent the team there."

"So what I'm saying is maybe you should go oversee that investigation, Detective Sheffley."  Spencer shook his head as he pulled Sharky's address for the newbie detective.  "We don't know for a fact that the car is Sharky's. Could be parked out front of Tigre's apartment even as we speak."

Sheffley's eyes widened as he realized the truth in Spencer's words. He grabbed the address from Spencer and bolted out of the room.

Spencer shook his head. "Amateurs," he muttered.

As Sheffley drove to Tigre's apartment complex, he called in Sharky's description as a person of interest wanted in connection with two murders. This way, if he's pulled over for a routine traffic stop or gets caught doing something stupid, they can bring Sharky to Sheffley instead of the other way around.

Eventually, criminals always screw up.

He parked in front of the beige, decrepit apartment building where Victor Cruz most likely lost his life. Crime scene tape cordoned off apartment number 135. Forensics team members moved around like ants, busily collecting samples—bagging and tagging.

He approached the scene and flashed his badge.

He'd seen Gina do it that morning and figured it was smart.  They would just ignore him otherwise.  To the uniform standing post he said, "I'm Detective Sheffley. This is my scene."

Wordlessly, the officer stepped aside and let him past the tape.  But he didn't get far.

"Wait!"  A man covered in protective gear waved a hand at Sheffley.  "You can't come in without covering up.  You'll contaminate the scene."

Sheffley instantly felt stupid, and he really didn't want to get dressed up like a surgeon.  He didn't need to *see* anything.  "I just want an update.  Anything good?"

"Uh, yeah.  This place is a gold mine," the forensics investigator said.  "We can't confirm a positive match to the victim until we're back at the lab, but there is definitely a crime scene here.  The apartment lit up like a Christmas tree under the luminol."

"Perp is already in custody for assaulting me," Sheffley confirmed.  "But this will help get justice for the family."

The investigator nodded.  With his shower cap, gown and booties, Sheffley had the hardest time taking him seriously.  He hoped he'd never have to wear a clown suit like this.

"We also found drugs, fingerprints, multiple hairs, and over a hundred thousand in cash," the forensics investigator added.

Sheffley's eyes widened at that.  They were going to have Tigre by the balls, at least.  "Great.  Let me know when you've I.D.'d the blood and hair samples."

With a final nod from the investigator, Sheffley wandered back to the parking lot.  He scanned quickly but didn't see any black Honda Civics anywhere.  He walked to the street corner and looked up and down.  Nothing.  There were a lot of junky cars and the whole area made Sheffley's skin crawl, but his dreams of easily stumbling across the car used in the other murder were soon squashed.

Hanging his head, he sauntered back to his car. He knew he hadn't been doing this for decades like Gina, but when he had dreamed of working homicide, he'd imagined the work being a lot more heroic. Digging in databases and waiting for crime lab reports was boring. Maybe he should have just stuck with being a beat cop.

And he knew Gina didn't like him. She was pretty and intimidating and despite his best judgment, he'd really wanted to impress her this morning. That had gone awry.

He'd been brutally honest with Internal Affairs after the altercation with Tigre and he'd expected suspension—or worse—for his conduct. But for some reason, he was getting another chance and he wanted to make this one count.

If he could prove Victor was murdered at the apartment, and if he found the car that killed Ethan, she'd have to at least respect his potential, hadn't she?

He sighed heavily as he climbed in his car.

And then he screamed.

Sitting in his passenger seat was Victor Cruz, pale with a twinge of blue, and four holes in his chest and abdomen, just like when they'd seen him this morning on the gurney.

"Wha… wha…" He couldn't form words. He'd never seen a ghost before, but he knew that's what was sitting with him. He could feel the sweat forming on his brow and the panic threatening to overtake him. He wanted to look around and see if anyone else could see it, but he didn't dare take his eyes off the apparition in his passenger seat.

Victor turned his head slowly toward Sheffley. He didn't speak. He didn't even open his grim mouth. Just raised his right hand.

And pointed.

Sheffley swallowed hard, trying to let reason control his actions. He was failing. But on autopilot he followed Victor's pointed blue finger and it led his eyes to the street.

"The car?" Sheffley looked back to Victor's ghost and then winced. Was he really talking to a ghost? What was happening right now? But Victor nodded in response and for some reason, that jolted Sheffley.  "You know where the car is?  The black Honda Civic that murdered Ethan Bender?"

Victor's ghost nodded again, still pointing to the street.

Sweat was still beading Sheffley's brow, and it wasn't just because they were in a car on a hot Fresno day.  He was on the borderline between madness and reason, and he assumed he was losing his mind completely.  But he really wanted to find that car and his instincts told him to follow the pointing dead finger.

So he turned the key, backed out, and drove in the direction Victor pointed.  When they got to the light, Victor pointed right.  Sheffley turned.  Another block and Victor pointed and he turned again.

"I'm telling no one about this," Sheffley muttered to himself.

Victor pointed forward and Sheffley immediately saw the heaps of junk everywhere.  A junkyard.

"Is this it?" Sheffley turned to ask Victor, but the

passenger seat was now empty. For some unknown reason, this made Sheffley's heart pound harder. He would panic, overthink everything that had just happened, and argue with himself about whether or not he was insane later. But right now he didn't have time.

Right before his eyes was a stripped-down black Honda Civic.

With shaking hands and a wavering voice, Sheffley called Gina. "I think I found the car that killed Ethan Bender."

# 14.

"This is the alleyway where Daniella was attacked." Daphne gestured behind the pawn shop as she and Gina rounded the corner. It was narrow, with loose gravel crunching beneath their feet. The far end was barricaded by buildings and two large dumpsters.

"Back there." Ethan pointed. "By the dumpsters."

Daphne rolled her eyes. "What a lovely place to be cornered. The ambience is just marvelous."

"It's where she would have been left for dead if I hadn't come along," Ethan explained. And as he did, an image of a young woman with long, black hair lying next to the dumpster came unbidden into her mind. She knew that was the alternate fate for Daniella.

She was lucky to be alive.

"Daphne!"

At the sound of her name, Daphne turned to see Miguel enter the alley with the same young woman whose dead body had flashed into her mind's eye.  It was pleasant, for once, to see an image like that followed by a living and breathing version of the same person.  It was a rarity, to be sure.

"Daniella," Daphne whispered as the girl came into view.

"Ms. Santos, I am Detective Gina Malone, working on two separate homicide cases where the perps are believed to also be the ones who attacked you.  I'm sorry to have to bring you back to such a traumatic place, but your statement could help us lock these two away for a very long time. Are you able to recount what happened that night?"

Daniella's large, frightened eyes moved from Gina to Daphne, where she zeroed in with a pleading look.

Daphne was rarely the person anyone turned to for support, so she was awkward at best, but she felt obligated to support this young victim.  Her life's work had been to fight for those who couldn't speak for themselves anymore, but this girl had only been a moment away from being a ghost herself.

So Daphne reached a hand out and rubbed Daniella's shoulder.  "It's okay.  They can't hurt you anymore. We just need to know what happened."

"I never went to the police.  So someone must have told you."  Daniella spoke with a clear, strong voice, despite the fear in her eyes.  "But Detective Alvarez explained that this is for the young man who saved me that night. The boy who died."

"That's correct, Ms. Santos."  Gina spoke calmly.  "I am investigating his murder.  He saved you and then died at your attacker's hands.  So this is your chance to get the young man justice."

For some reason, Daniella kept her eyes locked

on Daphne's as she finally gathered the courage to tell her story. Daphne knew it wasn't so much that she didn't want to tell the authorities, as it was that she was afraid that saying it out loud would make it real. She was coping by convincing herself it hadn't been real.

Daniella swallowed hard and then said, "I was walking home from work. I work at The Grille on the corner. I got off at midnight and began the short walk home. It had been a hot day, but the night air was pleasant. I remember thinking that. Isn't that funny?"

Daphne shook her head. The way Daniella stared at her it made her feel like they were the only two in the alley. Just two ladies talking, recounting a story from a recent evening. "It's very normal to remember simple thoughts like that when you encounter trauma."

"I didn't even know they were there. The two guys that grabbed me. My eyes were ahead of me, and from the darkness of the alley, arms appeared and pulled me in. I started to scream but they covered my mouth. One of them had a knife."

"Did you get a good enough look at the attackers?  Would you be able to identify them in a line-up?"

Daniella shook her head.  "In the alley, definitely not.  All I could think about was getting away from the knife.  But when the teenager showed up, it was like they forgot about me.   Like they were in a trance or something.  They decided to attack him instead and... and..."  Her eyes welled up with tears and her throat tightened.

But she didn't need to say it.  Daphne knew that emotion almost better than any other.

"She feels guilty for running away and leaving him to die at their hands," Daphne explained to Gina and Miguel.  She turned back to Daniella, who was fighting back emotion and still clinging to Daphne for emotional support.  "But you don't need to feel guilty.  You were supposed to live that night.  God chose to save you."

"Tell her who I am, Daphne," Ethan whispered.

"That boy you saw.  That night.  He wasn't just a

teenager who died from an attack by a couple of thugs." Daphne grabbed Daniella's hands and squeezed. "He was your guardian angel. And he did his job that night to save you."

"My guardian angel?" Daniella's voice was barely more than a whisper. But she seemed to be accepting Daphne's words, so Daphne continued.

"You have unfinished work and you've been given another chance. Everything you do from here on out should be for the glory of God." Daphne turned to Ethan. She had never talked about God before and yet all of a sudden he was a central character in her spiritual reading with Daniella. "Did you put those words in my mouth?"

Ethan just smiled.

"So you see, Daniella?" Miguel said. "You are very special and it was no accident you were saved that night. Is there anything else you can tell us? Anything at all that will help us lock those two characters up for good?"

Daniella turned to Miguel and nodded. "I saw

them run over that boy.  I hid over there behind that bush and watched them chase him down in their car.  A black car."

Miguel looked at Gina and she nodded, saying, "We have an eyewitness who corroborates Ethan's story. And Sheffley thinks he found the car.  Now we just need to find Sharky and have her ID them in a line-up."

Miguel squeezed the young girl's shoulder. "Thank you, Daniella.  I know this was scary to relive.  But your story is an important piece of getting justice for Ethan."  He spared a glance at Daphne.  "Your guardian angel."

"Can you leak this to the press?  I want my mom to know the real story.  And Daniella confirms it's all true."  Ethan was still smiling, but there was a pleading behind his angelic eyes.  No matter what his purpose was, he'd had a real mother who loved him and whom he'd loved in return.

Daphne sighed.  "No.  I'm not talking to the press."

Miguel and Gina ignored her, used to her quirks of talking to spirits they couldn't see. But Daniella asked, "What?"

"I'm talking to Ethan." She turned to the seemingly empty air. "I'm not talking to the press. I'll just go straight to your mom. Give me your human address."

Miguel leaned in to Daniella's confused face. "She's psychic. You get used to it."

Daniella nodded at Daphne. "So that's how you knew he was my guardian angel." It wasn't a question.

Daphne snorted. "He keeps announcing it."

"Was it..." Daniella started and then looked nervously at her feet. "Was it just that once, or is he, like, my actual guardian angel?"

Daphne looked at Ethan for the answer.

Ethan grabbed Daniella's hands, although she didn't know it. "I'm her guardian angel. I'll be there when she's in danger. And I'll be there when she's just feeling depressed. All she has to do is ask, and I'll always be there for her.”

Daphne shrugged.  “He says yes.  He’s your personal guardian angel.  So it must be nice to know you have one of those.”

“Daphne, you *all* do,” Ethan told her, but she kept that remark to herself.

And then Daniella surprised Daphne by throwing her arms around her neck.  “I knew it.  I knew someone was watching over me and I knew you were connected to it somehow.  Thank you.”

Daphne had never been one for public displays of affection.  It wasn’t that she hated it per se, she just wasn’t used to it.  At all.  So she awkwardly patted Daniella’s back, sensing her emotional tidal wave and knowing that she needed the embrace.

“I’m going to meet up with Sheffley about the murder weapon-slash-car,” Gina announced, shifting the moment back to the case.  “Come on, Daniella.  I can drive you home.  You’re my star witness.”  She turned to Miguel. “Call Spencer and see if you can track down

Sharky.  We need him brought in as soon as possible."

Miguel nodded.  "You got it, boss."  Gina winked and escorted Daniella to her car.

And then he turned to Daphne.  "You were great.  With Daniella.  You're getting better at handling people."

Daphne mulled his words over in her mind.  "Well, I think I've always been more understanding with victims.  It's just that I'm used to the victims I'm dealing with to be dead."

"Is that what you want to wear?"  Miguel pointed at her long skirt and boots.

Daphne looked down and then back at him, sensing a reason to be nervous.  "Yeah.  Why?"

"Because I'm taking you to my mom's house."

"Right now?"

Miguel nodded.

Daphne shrugged.  She didn't care what she was wearing and Miguel knew it.  She also was only nervous around her own parents.  She was comfortable around other people's parents.  And besides, from her intuition

Daphne already knew she liked Mrs. Alvarez. "Do *you* want me to change?"

Miguel stood there as the polar opposite to Daphne. Her short hair was pointing in every direction. She'd spent maybe half a second on it when she towel-dried it and let it go that morning. Miguel, on the other hand, had carefully put every hair in place and then gelled it there to keep it in place. He had been at a desk all day, so his clothes were still pristine and crisp. She had picked up a dirty T-shirt off the floor and been running around all day.

And still he shook his head. "I think you look perfect."

Daphne rolled her eyes. "Then why even ask?"

Miguel just laughed.

# 15.

The music was already blaring at the Alvarez household when Daphne and Miguel pulled up in the late afternoon.  Warm sun was baking through the window and creating a mini-oven.  But Daphne found that she really enjoyed the Fresno heat.  It was exhilarating in its own way.

"Do your parents always party like this?" Daphne asked Miguel as she turned to climb out of the car.

He smiled at her as he said, "Only on their anniversary."

Daphne rolled her eyes.  "Why didn't you tell me? I would've brought a gift."

"My parents have been married for thirty-eight

years.  They don't want gifts.  They want loved ones."  He climbed out of the car and Daphne followed.  Against the backdrop of a door slam, he smiled and said, "Besides, I thought maybe you already knew."

"Detective Miguel Alvarez.  Were you testing me? 'Cause that is a bad boyfriend move."

He walked around the car and scooped up her hand.  "No.  Not at all.  You just...tend to know things so sometimes I assume too much."

Daphne smiled back.  She looked at the white bungalow in front of her.  It was a simple, unassuming house, but she heard laughter and music coming from every crack and crevice.  This was a loving, happy home. "I get it.  Even I don't always know when or where I'm going to know something I shouldn't."

"Are you nervous?" Miguel asked.  He knew her relationship with her own movie star parents was rocky at best, even though she was trying to repair it.  He wanted to be sensitive to her having more parents to build a relationship with.  But he also really wanted his mom to know Daphne.  He struggled with the notion that she was his soulmate, but he had no choice but to accept that there was *something* about her.  He kissed the back of her hand, still entwined with his, as he waited for her answer.

Daphne shook her head.  "No.  I like your mom."

Miguel could only laugh.

"Is Ethan still around?"  Miguel asked as they continued toward the front door of his family home.

"Not at the moment."

"Did he cross over?  Or do angels even do that?" Miguel asked, truly curious.

Daphne shrugged.  "This is the first angel I've ever worked with.  But somehow I doubt it.  He strikes me as someone who will just always be around.  And anyway, his soul isn't finished until I talk to his mom."

Miguel nodded.  "I'll come with you when you do."

She squeezed his hand.  She knew that was the worst part of either of their jobs.  "You don't have to."

"I know," Miguel said as he opened the door and released a tidal wave of music. It was a song Daphne had never heard before. It had a techno beat and the singer was belting a rhythmic tune sung all in Spanish.

"Miguelito!" a chorus of voices announced as he walked through the front door. And then quickly all eyes went to the blonde trailing behind and clinging to his hand. Daphne had given up years ago on caring what people thought. It was exhausting for her to even try.

But she found that she actually wanted to be accepted by these people. A shy smile even crept across her mouth.

With a wave, Miguel whispered to Daphne, "Cousins." Then he continued on through the front room and into the kitchen.

It was a cozy kitchen with white countertops and a brick backsplash. It was a mix of old and classic in a way that said it had been updated as appliances and things had failed, more than a super expensive kitchen remodel. And Daphne loved that about what she saw and sensed as she entered the room.  It wasn't flamboyance.  It was decorated in a way that screamed practicality.

There were half a dozen women bouncing around hurriedly like ants at a picnic.  Rushing to the refrigerator.  Scampering to the stove.  Chopping at the island.  Scooping into serving dishes.

Miguel came up behind a woman much smaller than he was and swept her up into a giant embrace.  She screamed in delight when she realized who had just arrived at her party.

As he set his mother back down on her own two feet, Miguel stepped back to allow his two favorite women to see one another for the first time.  At least, the first time *physically*.  "Mami, I want you to meet Daphne, the love of my life."

If she thought too long about his words, Daphne might've panicked, but it felt so natural the way he said it that she knew it was fact.  And "girlfriend" really didn't describe their instant bond on any level.  And anyway, she had no time to analyze his introduction because

Miguel's mother beamed with joy and then ran to Daphne and squeezed her so tight Daphne had to gulp to get any air.

Daphne's own mother was fake. It was something Daphne struggled to reconcile. The fact that she was a professional actress had always somewhat embarrassed Daphne, even if she was Alanna Savage, the famous movie star. Her mother's profession had been something she'd tried to distance herself from to the point of almost denying her parentage at times.

But Miguel's mother was pure. She was real.

Daphne sensed it the moment they touched. It felt like this woman was everything she'd been running toward her whole life. Miguel's mother loved family, friends, and music. She put other people first and cared about their feelings. She admired honesty, even when it was hard to tell the truth.

"I've heard so much about you, querida," she said as she smoothed a couple of Daphne's hairs down in a motherly way. "I knew you were smart and psychic. But

Miguel barely scratched the surface in describing your beauty."

Daphne was taken aback by the compliment and spared a glance at Miguel.  He was full of love and admiration.  He didn't even try to hide it.

"And Miguel told me you were loving, but he barely scratched the surface in telling me how wonderful you are," Daphne countered with her own compliment.

Mrs. Alvarez waved away the compliment and said, "I'm no different than anyone else."  She turned to the feast of food behind her littering the tops of counters and grabbed a nearby plate.  It wasn't a paper plate, either, and that surprised Daphne. "Here.  Eat."

Daphne accepted the plate and Miguel leaned in. "Food.  It's her love language."

As if on cue, Daphne's stomach rumbled and she realized she'd spent the whole day solving Ethan's murder.  She had never stopped to eat and she was starving. "That's fine with me."

When Miguel and Daphne had piled their plates

to nearly overflowing, Mrs. Alvarez led them outside to a patio table.  There was a small gathering of men near a smoking barbecue and Mrs. Alvarez gestured to them. "Go grab your papi."

With a wink to Daphne, Miguel laid his plate down and obediently followed his mother's instructions. Mrs. Alvarez, meanwhile, sat down with Daphne.

"Miguel tells me you sometimes talk to my sister, Lencha."  Mrs. Alvarez tried to appear nonchalant, but Daphne knew she was fishing for a reading.  Normally, that might bother her, but feeling the acceptance of her gift without judgment was far outweighing anything else.

"She comes to me from time to time.  She watches over Miguel," Daphne answered honestly.

"Does she ever tell you…anything about me?" Mrs. Alvarez had the pain of grief in her eyes.  Even without sensing her emotions, Daphne knew that look.

Daphne shook her head and said, "She only *talks* to me about Miguel.  She knows about our bond."  At Mrs. Alvarez's obvious disappointment, Daphne placed a hand over hers. "But I know she loves you, too. And she's sorry she had to leave you so early, but she wants you to know she's in no pain. There's no more suffering."

"But she tells you this without words?"

Daphne nodded. "Sometimes I just *feel* the truth. No words are needed. Like how you met your husband when you were working at a diner. You wrote your phone number on his bill."

Mrs. Alvarez beamed. "I did. It's true. And not even Miguelito knows that I was the one to make the first move. Hector and I always kept that between us." She punctuated her sentence with a conspiratorial wink.

Daphne chuckled at that. There was nothing about the woman in front of her that cast any doubt that she would be the aggressor in the relationship, but people didn't always ask for those kinds of details. From Miguel's perspective, his parents just always were together. He'd never questioned its origins.

"Happy anniversary, by the way," Daphne responded.

"Daphne, this is my dad."  Miguel gestured to the older, but very similar man standing next to him.  His skin was a bit more weathered and there were lines around his eyes from years of laughing and squinting in the bright Central Valley sun, but there was no mistaking that this man was Miguel's father.

"Mucho gusto," Hector said, lifting Daphne's hand and kissing it like a scene from a movie.

"Mucho gusto," Daphne responded, the words fumbling in her mouth.  She made a mental note to brush up on her Spanish.  Her pronunciation was making her feel extra blonde at the moment.

"Daphne is so intuitive that she knew without me telling her that I brazenly gave you my phone number that fateful day at Otilio's," Mrs. Alvarez told her husband with a huge grin.  Daphne felt her chest tighten at the prospect that this woman she had just met was bragging about her.  Instead of being offended, Mrs. Alvarez was proud.

Miguel pulled a chair out next to Daphne and

moved it closer to her before he sat.  "Don't let her fool you, Mom.  Daphne chased me first, too."  He winked at Daphne as he put an arm possessively around her shoulder, and Daphne felt her face flush.  Pride, love, acceptance.  These were feelings as foreign to her as the Spanish she had stumbled over.

And she had always wanted to feel them.

"A strong woman knows what she wants and goes after it," Mrs. Alvarez said directly to Daphne.

Mr. Alvarez sat next to his wife and spoke in a very soft, calm voice.  "Men who don't respect a strong woman are the ones who suffer."

"Don't worry, Papi," Miguel said, dipping a piece of tortilla into his beans.  "I have no choice but to respect Daphne.  She knows what I am thinking anyway."  He tossed the bite of food into his mouth.

"But you know me too," Daphne responded.  She thought about the times when he knew to back off, or when he knew she was hurting.  He may not be psychic, but he was intuitive with her.  "You don't have to be psychic to respect someone."

"Words of wisdom," Papi said.

"Just out of curiosity, who is the man in your life who died young?" Daphne blurted.  She was already comfortable enough with the Alvarez family that she hoped this wouldn't scare them off.  "There is someone who has been with you since you first came over here."

Miguel looked at his papi questioningly.

But his mother looked at her husband like she knew.  Like they both knew.

Papi cleared his throat.  "His name was Cesar.  We grew up together.  Thick as thieves."  He laughed and shook his head at some distant memory both painful and joyful to remember.  "We used to do everything together.  I was with him at the diner when I met Andrea."  He nodded toward his wife and she confirmed it with a nod of her own.  "In 1991, he was at the bank depositing his paycheck when some *pendejos* came in to rob the place.  Everyone says he complied with their orders.  Everyone says he did nothing to provoke anything.  And the bank robbers only shot and killed one person that day."

"Cesar," Daphne stated.

"Cesar," Hector confirmed.

"Oh, Papi, I had no idea you'd lost your best friend in such a violent way," Miguel said, truly shocked at his father's painful memory.

"He has never left your side," Daphne told Hector.  "His spirit has been with you all these years." And then Daphne leaned in to get a better look at the spirit of Cesar standing right behind Miguel's father. "Wait.  Did he possibly sacrifice himself that day to save someone?"

"I don't actually know, but it's possible," Hector explained, a little bit of surprise in his tone.  "Not only was it truly his character, but supposedly there was a young man who was being a bit belligerent and everyone wondered why it was Cesar who'd been shot instead of that man."

"I know why," Daphne said.

"What are you seeing, Daph?" Miguel asked.

Daphne turned to Miguel. "Cesar has a golden aura. Just like Ethan."

Miguel smiled and nodded as realization dawned on him. "That's actually really beautiful."

"What? What is it?" Andrea Alvarez asked her son and Daphne. "That's good, right?"

"Yes, it's good," Daphne explained. "It means Cesar wasn't just anybody. He is a guardian angel. It was his life purpose to save that young man that day. And now he watches over you. All of you."

Miguel's parents exchanged a look before Mrs. Alvarez said, "Amazing."

"I told you, didn't I?" Miguel asked. "She's unbelievable."

Mrs. Alvarez reached across the table and grabbed Daphne's hands. "To be able to give people clarity and peace? What a beautiful gift. Miguel had told us you were very talented, but to see it in action? How extraordinary."

"Oh, my gawd," Daphne exclaimed. "That's it!"

"What, Daph?" Miguel asked.

"Is there somewhere more quiet we can go?" Daphne asked Miguel, but at the raised eyebrows across the table she quickly added, "Not for that.  I know how to find Sharky."

"A murderer I am trying to catch," Miguel explained to his parents.  He turned to Daphne.  "And how is that, honey?"

"Your mom reminded me.  I have *many* talents."

# 16.

"This is the best I can do without telling guests to leave."  Mrs. Alvarez had escorted Daphne and Miguel to a back bedroom.

"That's fine.  It doesn't have to be silent.  I just have to be able to concentrate," Daphne explained.

"Is there anything else you need?" Mrs. Alvarez asked.

Daphne shook her head.  "Everything I need is inside my head."

"You can close the door, Mami.  I'm not leaving her," Miguel explained, his eyes glued to Daphne.  There was enough worry on his face that his mother also had a nagging sense of concern.

"I don't know what you are doing, but if it is dangerous I am sure there is another way," Mrs. Alvarez said.

"It's always dangerous to go into the mind of a murderer," Miguel said with a tone of anger. Not at Daphne, but at the fact that this even needed to be done. That the world was so dark that Daphne had to ever enter dark minds like this.

"I'm always in control," Daphne told Mrs. Alvarez. She grabbed Miguel's hand and squeezed. "Always."

Miguel pressed his forehead against Daphne's. "I know."

The truth was he trusted her. He'd seen her in action multiple times now and had witnessed her power and talent firsthand. He knew she didn't need his protection. But it didn't stop him from worrying. It didn't prevent him from feeling a little bit helpless that he couldn't protect the one person in the world he wanted to protect most of all.

Mrs. Alvarez watched Miguel and Daphne and

her intuition gave her a sense of dread.  She was clueless to Daphne's methods of finding Sharky, but if Miguel was worried it was enough for her to worry also.  "I'm staying too."

"You're both worry warts."  Daphne rolled her eyes, but secretly she loved having them there.  She didn't really want them to worry, but the fact that they did was feeding a need deep down that she had pretended for years didn't exist.  She'd never admit it out loud, but the fact that they cared was sparking a little flame in her soul.

Daphne sat on the edge of the queen-sized bed and it squeaked a bit under her weight.  Miguel and Mrs. Alvarez remained standing, hovering really.  With a click of the bedroom door, Mrs. Alvarez leaned her weight against it and watched quietly.  Miguel stayed always within arms' reach just in case.  In case of what, he had no idea, but he felt better being close to Daphne.

Daphne closed her eyes and reached out psychically in search of Sharky.  It was impossible for her to explain with words what she was doing.  She just did it.  Reaching out over time and space?  She had no idea.  But she was searching for a connection to the murderer.  Digging through memories and psyches, hunting for Sharky the only way she knew how.

But there were over a million people in greater Fresno County.

Daphne shook her head.  "I might need Ethan.  I need something to guide me to the right person or I could be here all day."

"How do we call him?" Miguel asked.  He would do whatever Daphne needed.

"Looks like we just did."  Daphne stared into the corner of the bedroom where only she could see the young angel standing.

"I'll take you to him," Ethan said and vanished.  He knew instinctively what Daphne needed.  And she knew to follow him with her mind.

And with Ethan as her spirit guide, she found Sharky within minutes.  He didn't look like what she expected.  Hollywood always had thugs looking like thugs. But sometimes, they just looked like ordinary Joes.  That's what Sharky reminded Daphne of.  If he walked into the store behind her, she wouldn't think anything of it.  She would never jump to the conclusion based on looks that this guy was a murderer and a felon.

But the minute she saw him, she knew.  She knew with perfect clarity that he had been in the alley when Daniella was attacked.  He'd held the knife to her throat. He drove the car that ended Ethan's life.  He was the mastermind behind Victor Cruz's "hit" cover-up.  He was a career criminal.

"I've got him," Daphne announced.

Mrs. Alvarez actually gasped at what she was witnessing.

"Where do I tell the cops to go pick him up?" Miguel asked, his phone in his hand.

Daphne shook her head.  "No need.  I'm taking him to you."

And as she had done with Stryker in Southern

California, she took a deep breath and went straight into Sharky's mind.

The feeling in Sharky's mind was vastly different than Stryker's. Stryker had gotten off on power and it had turned him dark in a truly evil way. Sharky was different. Sharky was a survivor. He had lived a hard life on the streets and had learned the hard way that it was kill or be killed. It had also turned him dark inside, but it wasn't out of desire to do harm as much as desire to not *be* harmed.

And either way, Daphne didn't really care. He was a murderer that she wanted brought to justice.

Sharky was sitting between a couple of lackeys. He would call them friends, but Daphne knew that Sharky didn't actually have any of those. He had people he could use again and again. But he would discard them the minute they became useless to him. And those were the people he called friends.

Daphne took control of Sharky's mind and forced him to say, "I'm out, guys. I'm turning straight."

The lackeys he was hanging out with began to laugh. They naturally assumed he was joking. No one had taught them more about the life of crime than Sharky had. Turning legit was inconceivable.

And leaving them to assume it was giant practical joke, Daphne forced Sharky to pick up his keys and march to his car parked in the driveway. He was pretty consistent in his method of dumping cars and procuring new ones. He'd never actually purchased a car in his life. After the Civic they'd used to rundown Ethan, Sharky had hotwired a white Toyota Corolla. Newbies would be attracted to something flashy, fast and red. But Sharky knew better. He knew to go with the car that would blend in.

And with his friends still laughing in the distance, Sharky climbed into the white car and turned the key in the ignition. He didn't seem to be pushing back on her at all. He had to be confused as to why he suddenly wanted to go to the police, but nonetheless he followed Daphne's psychic instructions and pulled out of the driveway, heading for the glass building that housed the police headquarters downtown.

As Daphne stayed with Sharky to ensure he made it all the way to the police, Miguel dialed Gina's number. He may not be her official partner at the moment, but he was her partner in spirit if nothing else.  And besides, he was doing deskwork on this case.

And so when Daphne forced Sharky to park the car and march into the building, that's how he found Sheffley and Gina right there ready to interrogate him the moment he passed through the glass double entryway doors.

"Sharky, I presume?" Gina asked, one hand on her hip.

"That's me!  I did it.  I'm ready to tell you everything," Sharky announced.  Gina would have laughed if Miguel hadn't filled her in on the fact that Daphne was using mind control to get him here.  His response was so joyful and over the top, that it made no sense in a comical way coming out of this street thug.

"We can't wait to hear it," Sheffley said as he grabbed Sharky's arm and led him toward the interrogation rooms.  Sharky would have been angry at being manhandled by cops, but with Daphne at the helm he was completely compliant.

When Sheffley, Gina and Sharky made it to their desired room, and Sheffley closed the door behind them, Gina leaned across the table and said in a soft voice, "Okay, Daphne. We've got it from here.  It doesn't really matter how much he admits it or not.  We have the evidence to arrest him.  Thank you."

Daphne made Sharky nod and then snapped back to Miguel's family's house.

"Got him.  Gina's questioning him now," Daphne explained.

With an overwhelming flood of relief, Miguel pulled Daphne up into his arms.  "You made that look easy."

Mrs. Alvarez came over and wrapped an arm around her son and Daphne.  "I don't know what I just witnessed, but I'm glad everything is okay."

Daphne huffed a laugh.  "He was actually pretty weak-minded.  Most people are."  And then realizing she might have been rude accidentally, she added, "No offense."

Miguel looked at his mom and they both laughed.

# 17.

"That's it.    My loving family home," Ethan explained to Daphne without a hint of sarcasm.    They stood out front of a beautiful brick house, located around the corner from Jake's house where the day before they had been talking to Ethan's best friend.

"You got to live in a fancy house in your short life," Daphne commented.

"I probably didn't appreciate it as much as I should have, but I was very blessed."  Ethan flashed his charismatic smile.

Daphne was used to talking to grieving family members with enraged or heartbroken ghosts.  The smiling, calm angel next to her was a very different experience.  But she liked it.  There was a peacefulness that Daphne was very rarely allowed in her line of work.

"Shall we?" Daphne asked Ethan.

With a nod and a smile, Ethan answered, "We shall."

Daphne approached the front step, looking all around her at the home that would have greeted the young baseball player every day when he was alive. There was a large, standing welcome sign and flowers decorating the porch.  It was clean, as if someone took a blower to it regularly.  Not even cobwebs hid out in the dark corners.  The front door was painted black and provided the backdrop for a wreath of large, brightly colored flowers.

Through the front window, Daphne could see a beautiful woman with her hair pulled into a low ponytail. Her face was tanned and riddled with the lines that Daphne knew came from tremendous loss.  She was standing over a sink and rinsing a plate.

"Your mother is very pretty," Daphne said.

"Oh, she is," Ethan agreed.  "And even more so, her soul is beautiful.  It's no accident who gets chosen to raise angels."

The way he said it sounded like a boast or hyperbole, but Daphne knew it wasn't.  This woman had been the right person to partner with the angelic soul of Ethan Bender, the young man who was destined to sacrifice his own life for a stranger's.

Steeling herself for the job she was here to do, Daphne raised a hand and knocked.

Mrs. Bender looked up from her sink to see who was calling unannounced in the middle of the day.  She dried her hands on a nearby towel and answered the door.

"Can I help you?" Mrs. Bender asked.

"Hi, Mrs. Bender.  You don't know me, but I know your son, Ethan."  Daphne stole a glance at the spirit beside her and he was beaming with joy and pride.

The words were painful to Mrs. Bender.  She physically recoiled from the mention of the son she was still grieving.  But she said nothing, just waited for Daphne to explain further.

Daphne didn't care if she was invited in or not. She could do this on the front porch.  She had done that many a time before.  So she just dove right in.  "I am a psychic medium and a consultant for the Fresno P.D., Homicide division."

Daphne let that simmer with Mrs. Bender for a moment.  The grieving mother just folded her arms across her chest and waited for Daphne to get to the point.

"Ethan did not commit suicide.  We have multiple witnesses who can attest that he was run over by a car before being dumped over the overpass.  Not accidentally, either."

Mrs. Bender softened a bit at the prospect that her hunch had been right all along, but she was still guarded.  The pain at having this news dangled before her and then finding out it was all a joke or something was swirling around her mind.  "I know he didn't commit suicide.  But who would want to run him over with a car? It makes no sense."

"Mrs. Bender, Ethan interrupted an attack on a young girl.  He knew they would turn their malicious attentions on him, but he went in any way.  Your son's a hero.  He saved a young girl's life that night.  And paid for it with his own."

The tears began to pool in Ethan's mother's eyes. She knew how wonderful her son was.  Maybe even proud that he was a hero.  But she still hated the fact he'd been taken from her.  "How do you know all this?"

"Daniella Santos.  She's the young girl whose life he saved.  She witnessed the whole thing, including when the two men chased and then ran down Ethan with their car.  We have both men in custody and the car they used to kill Ethan.  You're going to get justice, Mrs. Bender."  It was the best Daphne could offer her right now.

Mrs. Bender sighed.  "I guess that's good.  But it doesn't bring him back."

"No, it doesn't."  Daphne frowned.  She could feel

the sadness radiating off the woman in front of her, and it was enough to swallow you whole.  Her joyous world had been flipped upside down and barely made sense anymore.

It was painful enough to lose someone you love to natural causes.  But to know someone had ended their life maliciously added another layer of emotional injury.

And then Mrs. Bender locked eyes with Daphne. "But you said multiple witnesses?  Besides the young woman, Daniella, who else knows the full story?"

"Tell her."  Ethan leaned in to Daphne.  "Tell her everything.  Let her know who I am.  She deserves to know."

Since she was young, Daphne had always known that she was different from other people.  Sometimes it was plain weird and off-putting.  But sometimes it helped people, especially people who were being swept away in the current of their grief.  Ethan was barely even a ghost to Daphne anymore, but she knew to the woman in the doorway he would always just be the young man with the charismatic smile.    He would forever be her baby. Ethan's mother had hopes and dreams for the child she'd raised, and those were cut short by a deal that was made before she'd ever given birth.

"The other witness is your son, Ethan."  Daphne watched Mrs. Bender to see if she would push back, be angry at Daphne for again allowing her to hope that her son's soul lived on.  "He's been with me the past few days, helping me uncover the truth."

"You've seen my baby?"  The tears began to well again.

Daphne nodded slowly.  "He's still here, Mrs. Bender."

"Please.  You can call me Olivia."

"That's a good sign," Ethan said, squeezing Daphne's shoulder.

"And he's here with me now, still smiling and jolly like always."  Daphne turned to the young man next to her, allowing Olivia Bender the chance to know where he was, even if she couldn't see him.

Mrs. Bender walked forward and through her son.  She breathed deeply, feeling around for his soul.  She smiled through her tears and seemed to accept that he was truly there.

"Tell her I hate chocolate cake.  That way she'll know for sure," Ethan said to Daphne.

"He wants me to tell you about how he hates chocolate cake.  Does that mean anything to you?" Daphne asked.

Mrs. Bender laughed.  "Yes.  He was always the biggest weirdo in his loathing for chocolate cake."

"And I know he loved baseball and had a best friend named Jake.  And was always happy, confident and smiling.  I don't like that he had to die that night any more than you do, but it was meant to be, as hard as that is to accept.  Because there's even more."

Mrs. Bender slowly turned from feeling for her son and back toward Daphne.  "Yes?"  She said it hesitantly, like the next news might cause a fissure that would send her heart into a pile of rubble.

"He saved Daniella's life that night because it was his job."  Daphne also spoke carefully.  "He was no ordinary boy, Olivia.  Your son, Ethan, is a guardian angel.  When he was given the chance to live as a human, he agreed to sacrifice himself to protect others."

"An angel?  So Ethan wasn't my son?"  Mrs. Bender shook her head, unable to fully grasp the meaning of this new information.  She didn't reject it outright either, so Daphne remained hopeful.

"Of course I'm your son, Mom."  Ethan grabbed his mother's hand, even if she couldn't feel it.

"He's both, Olivia.  He's your son, who is an angel.  And not in the metaphoric way we refer to children.  You were raising an angel. Literally."  Daphne smiled, hoping it might comfort the heartbroken mother.

Her voice barely more than a whisper, Mrs. Bender said, "My son is an angel."

Daphne could feel her sorrows receding, the tidal wave of grief beginning to ebb at this new revelation.

"And it was no accident that you were chosen to

be his mother, or so he tells me.  That means you're pretty special, too," Daphne explained.

Mrs. Bender looked up at Daphne, as if she was unsure that that was a fair conclusion.  She knew she was lucky to have been a part of such a great person's life, but special enough to be chosen as the mother of an angel?  Harder to accept.  "So if he's a guardian angel, does that mean he will always be around guarding people?  What does any of this you're telling me mean?"

Daphne took the risk and reached out to squeeze Olivia Bender's hand.  She knew Ethan's mother just needed the world to make sense.  Her heart would never be whole again, but she could begin to heal if the picture at least came into focus.  Mrs. Bender didn't pull away.  At this moment, Daphne was the lifeline to her son.

"Usually, my job is to provide closure, for both the spirit and the living people left behind," Daphne explained.  "But Ethan is no ordinary spirit.  He's not going to cross over.  He has a job to do, watching over us, keeping us safe.  What all this means, Mrs. Bender, is that your son may have had a brief life in a physical body, but as an angel he'll never leave this world.  Spiritually, you've lost *nothing*."

Mrs. Bender mulled over Daphne's words.  "But how will I see him?  If he's here, how can I know?  I want to talk to him."

Ethan nudged the psychic.  "Let me take this one, Daphne."

She nodded and gestured for him to respond to his mother.  And Daphne watched as he began to glow brightly there on his own front porch, his spirit lighting up like a decoration on a Christmas tree.  Olivia Bender smiled through the tears that she could no longer contain. She could see the golden glow in front of her.

"Mom."  Ethan spoke with a voice that was loud and clear to Daphne, muffled and distant to Olivia.  But she could hear him.  She recognized the voice. And it was enough.  "All you ever have to do is call my name.  I am always with you.  And when you or Dad are scared or worried or feeling helpless, look for me.  You can have faith that it will be all right because I am protecting you."

"How are you always here but also always with Daniella?  Just curious on how it works," Daphne asked.

Ethan flashed his smile.  "I'm not a human ghost, Daphne.  I'm an angel.  Watching over many all at once is what I do."

Daphne shrugged.  Helping an angel solve their own murder was a first for Daphne, but no one knew better than she that the physical world and the spiritual world were nothing alike.  The concepts and preconceived notions that we all held just didn't hold up when it came to angels and ghosts.  She may not have understood it fully, but she could accept that Ethan was in multiple places at once fulfilling his role as a guardian angel.

"Ethan?  Baby?"  Olivia Bender reached out to the glowing being before her.

"I'm right here, Mom.  I'm always right here."  Ethan reached out to his mother and touched her with a glowing hand.

Mrs. Bender smiled.  "I can feel him."

"I know I've given you a lot to process, Olivia," Daphne said.  "But at least you now know Ethan is still here with you.  You don't have to wonder and hope.  You *know*.  Believe me, that's more than many people ever get."

"I am very grateful to you, Daphne.  Thank you for coming here and telling me."  Olivia still stared at the glow before her even as she spoke to Daphne.

Daphne snorted.  "Trust me, Ethan wouldn't have let me keep it to myself even if I had wanted to.  He wanted you to know everything."

Olivia laughed through her tears, imagining her persevering son continuously nagging Daphne until she gave in.

"Oh.  One more thing."  Daphne reached into her pocket and pulled out two business cards.  "For details on the homicide case, call Detective Gina Malone or Detective Miguel Alvarez.  They can fill you in on the latest."

Olivia took the cards and put them in her pocket. "I'm not sure I need to know a lot of details, but I suppose it will give me comfort to know the murderers are put behind bars."

"The world is definitely a safer place now with those two put away, believe me," Daphne agreed.

Olivia smiled a genuine smile. "And with my son protecting us all."

Daphne smiled back. "Yeah. He's the first angel I ever knew."

Mrs. Bender turned to her son, whose glowing hand still held her own. "My son is an angel."

And Daphne felt, as much as saw, that this realization did help. A tiny piece of her fractured heart was made whole again knowing that she had someone watching over her. And not just anyone: her son, the guardian angel Ethan Bender.

# 18.

"Put your feet down," The Sarge bellowed at Detective Gina Malone.

She removed her feet from her desk with a loud flop, and a big smile.  She drew great pleasure from pushing that particular button.

"And you three," he said, pointing at Gina, Miguel and Sheffley.  "Nice work on the Victor Cruz and Ethan Bender cases.  I love it when we close two cases at once.  And so does the D.A.  And so does the mayor."

The Sarge closed his door behind him as he walked back into his office.

Sheffley rolled his chair over to Gina and Miguel. He was lucky enough to get a desk right next to these two detectives he admired so much.  "We're a great threesome, huh?"

Gina rolled her eyes.  "Don't ever say those words out loud again."

"You did good, Sheffley," Miguel said with a smile.  "Even had your first ghostly encounter and didn't soil yourself."

"How did you know about that?"  Sheffley had sworn he would never tell another living soul about Victor Cruz's ghost.  He still had to talk himself into belief that it had happened.

"He's dating the psychic."  Gina pointed a thumb in Miguel's direction.  "Prepare to have no secrets."

"It's actually a perk to the job.  If you want a career in homicide, it's best to start talking to ghosts early and often," Miguel explained.

Gina leaned back in her chair and put her feet back up on the desk.  "As if you even believed in ghosts until you met Daphne."

Miguel didn't deny it.  "But you have to admit

that now that I do, we close these cases a lot faster than we ever did before."

Sheffley bit his lip and decided that it was okay to come clean with these two. "All right. It's true. I wouldn't have found that car without that ghost. It was awful, but it worked."

"What happened exactly?" Miguel asked.

Sheffley shrugged. "He appeared in my front seat and pointed where to go. Never spoke though."

Miguel looked at Gina, then back to Sheffley. "Hmm. I wonder why you can see ghosts. I never have. Without Daphne, I'd have no idea there was one even around."

Sheffley looked from Miguel to Gina. He had assumed the way they were talking that his experience had been sort of run-of-the-mill for these two. "What?"

Gina smiled. "Maybe you have the gift."

Miguel looked at the horrified and shocked face of the young detective. "The point is, when the victims tell you what happened, you'll be a better homicide detective.  If you can see them, that's a plus."

"Welcome to the team, Sheffley.  I think between you and Daphne seeing and talking to the victims, and me and Miguel being experienced detectives, we're going to close a lot of cases."  Gina smiled and folded her arms, her feet still propped on the desk the way The Sarge hated.  She had accepted her role as mentor to Sheffley.  Maybe even come to appreciate it and enjoy it a little bit.

In any case, the team did feel whole now.

"So, I've been thinking…"  Miguel hesitated, suddenly unsure what Gina would say.  He was open to taking Sheffley under his wing, but Gina had been his partner for a decade.  He trusted her as if she were family.

Her support meant everything to him.

"Why am I nervous at the sound of that?"  Gina raised an eyebrow.

"What do you think about switching to cold cases?"  It was out there now, so Miguel continued to just blurt his stream of consciousness.  "There are plenty of detectives to work active cases, but who fights for the families with no closure?  We have a tool not everyone has."

"And by tool you mean Daphne?"  Gina pursed her lips.

"I meant psychic powers." Miguel clarified.

"Your trip to Southern California really inspired you, huh?" Gina asked.

"A little bit.  I do have a complete admiration for Detective Cayman.  But it's more than that.  I'm talking about doing something no one else can do.  Closing cases with little to nothing to go on because we have the ghosts themselves guiding us.  We can make a real difference, Gina."

Gina dropped her feet to the ground, again letting the thud reverberate around the pit.  She loved distracting everyone around her as much as she loved annoying The Sarge. "Sounds good. I'm in."  She turned to Sheffley.  "What about you, rookie?  Willing to give cold cases a try?"

Sheffley pointed to his own chest, surprised again to be included in their version of "we."  "Uh, yeah.  Of course.  I'm in."

"Well, all right."  Miguel smiled and leaned back in his chair.  He hadn't expected it to be so easy.  Gina loved homicide and Sheffley was just starting his career there.  "I'll make the case to The Sarge."

"Detectives Malone, Alvarez and Sheffley.  Cold Case Division."  Gina smiled.  "Yeah.  I like the sound of that."

"Me too," Sheffley beamed.

"Yeah, me too," Miguel agreed.  "I think we're going to shake things up in a big way."

"And if I know you as I do, you already have a case picked out."  Gina smiled at her partner.

"As a matter of fact, Detective Malone, I do.  I guess I had a little too much time to myself in this desk job."  Miguel picked up a manila folder off his desk and dropped it on Gina's.  "Her name is Melissa Daniel.  She was a college student at Fresno State.  Last seen by her roommate on a cold wintry night in January 1989 as Melissa headed off to work.  She was a waitress at the Denny's at Shaw and First.  She left around 4pm for the dinner shift and was never seen again."

Detective Malone rifled through the file.  "Her body?"

Miguel shook his head.  "Never found.  Just her car, three days later covered in her blood.  Her family is still waiting for answers on what happened to her.  And closure."

"I'm intrigued, Miguel," Gina said and handed the file to Sheffley.

He took it willingly and said, "Thanks for including me, guys."

He was surprised at how much he wanted to be a part of this little group.  He knew he was coming across as an eager little brother, but it was so natural as to be almost endearing to Gina and Miguel.

Miguel nodded and Gina said, "It might have taken me a minute to be accepting, but you've proven yourself.  You're one of us now.  So let's use every talent in our arsenal to find Melissa Daniel and get justice for her family."

# 19.

"I brought you dinner."  Miguel stood in Daphne's doorway holding up a bag of burgers and fries.  The smell of French fries filled the air, swirling its way into Daphne's apartment.

With a smile, Daphne opened her door wide to let Miguel (and the food) in.  "I'm starving."

Miguel waltzed in, completely at home in Daphne's tiny apartment.  "I figured you might be.  It has to be taxing to talk to the families.  It always is for me."

He placed the bag on the table and began pulling out their food.

"Yeah, it can be.  But this time, Ethan's mom was really proud to have an angel for a son, so it took a bit of the sting off.  She might call you guys regarding the case. I gave her your card."  Daphne grabbed a fry and popped it into her mouth.

Miguel nodded.  It was part of the job and he accepted it willingly.

"Oh. Also. Can you help the non-profit Angels of Freedom get the knife out of the Westside Trade & Loan? It was Sharky's and I suspect it was used in both Daniella's attack and a murder where the wrong guy is sitting behind bars."

Miguel raised an eyebrow. "Is there a new ghost talking to you now?"

Daphne laughed. "Not this time. Just good ole fashioned justice." At Miguel's skepticism, Daphne added, "Tyra Cruz suggested it."

Miguel nodded and then sat down to eat.  And change the subject. "So Gina and I were actually thinking about switching to cold cases.  I'm going to talk to The Sarge about it tomorrow."

"I know," Daphne said nonchalantly.  "And don't

worry.  He's going to say yes.  It's where you were meant to end up."

Miguel laughed and shook his head.  He had gotten somewhat used to her knowing everything before he said it, and yet somehow it still always caught him off guard.  "And Gina is presenting the Victor Cruz and Ethan Bender homicides to the District Attorney's office tomorrow, so Sharky and Tigre will at least be off the streets. Two more murderers put away. Thanks to you."

Daphne shrugged and then took a giant bite of her hamburger.  She agreed with the sentiment that it was rewarding to see these guys punished for their crimes, but she never felt like self-congratulations were in order.  She chewed, swallowed and then said, "I didn't do anything you and Gina wouldn't do.  And Sheffley."  She leaned back.  "What's that guy's deal anyway?"

Miguel smiled with a wicked gleam in his eye and suddenly Daphne felt very self-conscious.  "What?" she said.

Miguel grabbed a napkin and wiped Daphne's

chin.  "It's hard to take you seriously with ketchup on your face."

Embarrassed, she picked up a fry and chucked it at Miguel, hitting him squarely in the face.  But it was playful and they both laughed.  Miguel even picked up the offending fry and ate it as a peace offering.

"Sheffley is just new.  And I think he might have a crush on Gina," Miguel explained.  And then he remembered how Sheffley had actually seen Victor Cruz's ghost.  "Hey, do you know if he's psychic at all?"

Daphne shrugged again as she popped another fry in her mouth.  "He's open-minded.  And he's eager.  You'd be surprised what those two features can get you in life."

"You say it as if *I'm* not open-minded or something."  Miguel smiled again, remembering how skeptical he was when Daphne first came into his life.

Daphne stared at him for a long time.  His gunshot wound had mostly healed, but he'd accepted his desk job duties with a grace Daphne was certain she could never muster.  In fact, any setting with an authority figure instantly made her want to rebel on principle alone.  And not only had he listened to evidence from ghosts on multiple occasions, but he was now choosing to make it his life's work by moving onto cold cases like her mentor, Winston Cayman.

And he'd embraced her and her gifts fully, even loved her for it and in spite of it.  This was not something Daphne encountered every day.  In fact, usually she was scaring people off—especially male suitors.

Open-minded was putting it mildly.  Miguel was a rare gift and Daphne told herself to be thankful.

She was never great with words and feelings, so instead of responding, she kissed Miguel on the cheek.

And changed the subject.  "She goes by Amber."

"Okay."  He might be used to this habit of Daphne's, but it didn't make him any more equipped to know what she was talking about.  "Who does?"

"Your cold case.  Melissa Amber Daniel.  If you start asking around about a Melissa Daniel, no one will know what you are talking about.  She went by her middle name."

Miguel stopped chewing.  "Good to know."  He gloated a little internally, because he knew he would be as great in cold cases as Cayman was.  And for the same reason: Daphne.  But even as he knew what a great team they were, he also knew she felt the same as he did.  It was about justice and closure for the victims and their families.  "I wonder if Amber's spirit is still hanging around?"

"She might be.  Especially if she was attacked or murdered.  As of right now, she's still just missing.  She could be alive.  And then there would be no ghost to talk to, Mr. Hoity-Toity Cold Case Detective."  Daphne smiled at the handsome, well-kempt man before her.

"Well, little Miss Fancy Pants Psychic Medium, it may surprise you, but I hope that is, in fact, the ending to our very first case.  That Amber Daniel is living a new life in Texas or somewhere."  Miguel leaned back in his seat.  "In fact, I hope that's the ending to every cold case I work on."

Daphne stood and walked over to where Miguel was sitting. "I know." She climbed in his lap and put her head on his chest. "But take it from me, Detective. There are fates much worse than death."


This story continues in Daphne Winters Psychic Investigation Series #4: *Vanished*